The Haunted Woman

The Haunted Woman

David Lindsay

MINT EDITIONS

The Haunted Woman was first published in 1922.

This edition published by Mint Editions 2021.

ISBN 9781513299853 | E-ISBN 9781513223551

Published by Mint Editions®

 MINT
EDITIONS

MintEditionBooks.com

Publishing Director: Jennifer Newens
Design & Production: Rachel Lopez Metzger
Project Manager: Micaela Clark
Typesetting: Westchester Publishing Services

Contents

I

MARSHALL RETURNS FROM AMERICA

In the latter half of August, Marshall Stokes went to New York, in order to wind up the estate of the lately-deceased brother of the lady to whom he was betrothed. As a busy underwriting member of Lloyd's, he could ill afford the time—he was over there for upwards of a fortnight—but no alternative had presented itself. Miss Loment had no connections in America, she possessed no other relations, except a widowed aunt, with whom she lived, and it was clearly out of the question for either of the two ladies to travel across in person, to examine books, interview lawyers, deal with claims, etc.—they had not the necessary business experience. The task, therefore, had devolved on Marshall. He had not been able to conclude the business, but he had put it in a fair way of being concluded, and had appointed a reputable firm to act as Miss Loment's representatives. The estate was worth forty thousand dollars.

Upon his return to London about the middle of September he found that his friends had departed for Brighton; Mrs. Moor—the aunt—apparently was feeling rundown. A perfumed little note from Isbel pressed him to join them there. Marshall was unable to leave town immediately, but two days later, on Friday afternoon, he abruptly shut down work for the week-end, and motored down by himself in glorious weather. His heart was high, and as he ran through the richly gleaming Sussex country, overspread with a blue, plum-like bloom, arising from the September mists, he thought that he had never seen anything quite so lovely. The sun was brilliant, and there was a crisp, invigorating breeze.

He dined the same evening with Isbel and her aunt, in the public room at the Hotel Gondy, where they were staying. Neither of the ladies attracted as much attention as Marshall himself. His large, loose, powerful figure went admirably with evening dress, while his full-blooded face, still covered with ocean tan, was peculiarly noticeable for its heavy, good-humored immobility; his very hands, huge and crimson, yet not vulgar, marked him out from other men. Isbel kept alternately glancing at him and smiling down at her plate with pleasure, apropos of nothing. Most of the talking came from him. Reserving business until afterwards, he entertained his friends during the meal with his personal experiences in the United States, the relation of which was rendered more piquant by a free adoption of the very latest slang. Aunt and niece were both perfectly acquainted with America, but they had the tact to keep this to themselves.

Isbel was dressed in black, on account of her brother's death. The gown, according to the prevailing fashion, was cut low across her somewhat full bosom, but lower still in the back. She was neither plain nor handsome; a first glance showed an ordinarily attractive girl of five-and-twenty, and nothing more. Her face was rather short and broad, with thick but sensitive features, a lowish forehead, and a dull, heavy skin, rendered almost unnaturally pale by the excessive quantity of powder she employed. The tranquillity of her expression was rarely broken by an emotion or a smile, but whenever this did happen it was like a mask lifting. The full, grey-black eyes as a rule appeared a trifle bored and absent, but occasionally they narrowed into a subtle and penetrating glance which nearly resembled a stab. Her hair was long and fine, but mouse-coloured. She was short, rather than tall, and somewhat too broad-hipped for modern ideas of beauty; nevertheless, her person was graceful and well-covered, she moved with style, while her hands and feet were particularly small and aristocratic. She affected little jewelry.

She commanded all her friends, and was adored by the two or three nearest to her. Further, no matter what company she was in, and although she never exerted herself to win people, before the evening was out her personality always succeeded in making itself felt, and she became the centre of interest to men and women alike. Never self-conscious, never embarrassed, always quiet and rather ennuye, she fascinated by the very strength of her silence, which, it was abundantly clear, had nothing in common with stupidity. She had already declined three offers of marriage, before Marshall had appeared on her horizon. Curiously enough, these offers had all been made by men very much older than herself.

She had a queer habit, while sitting, of constantly, though quite unconsciously, attending her person. She would keep putting her hand to her hair, adjusting her skirt, feeling her waist-band, altering the position of a necklace or bracelet, etc. It was not vanity, but a sort of nervous irritability, which prevented her from continuing still.

Her aunt frequently cautioned her against the fault, which was one of those that grow by indulgence; Isbel would deny the offence, and five minutes later would begin to repeat it. The strange thing was that a good many persons of the other sex liked to watch her toying with her garments in this way. She was perfectly well aware of the fact, and it rather disgusted her.

Mrs. Moor, the third member of the party, had just entered her sixtieth year. She was—as already mentioned—a widow. Her husband, a stockbroker in a small way, had during the rubber boom amassed a sudden fortune, which fell to her intact upon his death in 1911. By shrewd speculation she had increased it considerably since, and could now be regarded as a wealthy woman. Isbel's father, who had died nearly at the same time, was her younger brother. He was a widower, with only one other child, a son—the one who had recently died in New York. Isbel, who at that time was sixteen became Ann Moor's ward, under the will. She was at once removed from school—rather against her desire—and the two women commenced the more or less vagrant existence together, which they had continued ever since, drifting from hotel to hotel in all quarters of the globe. It was a free life, and Isbel came to grow extremely fond of it. In any case, her own money was not sufficient to support her, so that in a manner she was dependent upon her aunt's whims. It only remains to add that she tyrannised over the older woman in all her personal relations, and that the latter not only permitted this, but even seemed to expect it as a natural thing.

Mrs. Moor was short, erect, and dignified, with a somewhat stiff carriage. Her face, which resembled yellow marble, bore a consistently stern and dauntless expression, rarely relaxing into a smile. She was in complete possession of all her faculties, and her health, generally speaking, was good. The art of dressing she did not understand; Isbel selected her garments for her, while her maid told her when and how to put them on. She was, in fact, one of those eccentric women who ought to have been born men. Her tastes were masculine, her knowledge chiefly related to masculine topics. She knew, for instance, how to invest her money to the best advantage, how to buy and sell land, and how to plan a serviceable house; but what she did not know was how to flatter men, how to talk gracefully about nothing, how to interest herself in the minute details of another woman's household, or how to identify herself in thought with the members of the upper circles of society. She bowed to no authority, and took pride in speaking her mind in whatever company she might find herself. The natural consequence was that, while her friends esteemed her highly for her genuine qualities, they were more than a little frightened of her, and never really regarded her as one of themselves. It sometimes dawned on her that she was lonely. On such occasions she sought solace in music. She loved everything classical, Beethoven in particular she venerated, but the history of music came to an end, for her, with Brahms. Weeks would pass without her once opening the piano, and then a sudden, almost passionate yearning would seize her, when she would sit down and play by the hour together. Her execution was bold, slow, rather coarse, full of deep feeling.

The two women were excessively fond of each other, thought neither cared to show it. Temperamentally, however, they were so antagonistic that frequent quarrels were inevitable. Whenever this happened, the aunt ordinarily expressed herself in vigorous language, while Isbel, on the other hand, would become sullen and vindictive, saying little, but requiring time to be appeased.

As soon as dinner was concluded, the trio retired to Mrs. Moor's private apartment on the first floor. The waiter brought up coffee and Chartreuse. The room was handsomely appointed, a distinctive note being lent to it by the bowls of pale chrysanthemums with which it was profusely and artistically decorated—Isbel's labour of love. The evening was chilly, and a small fire was burning in the grate. They brought their chairs forward, so as to form a semi-circle round the hearth, Isbel being in the middle. She stretched a languid hand up, and took two cigarettes from an open box on the mantelshelf, passing one to Marshall and keeping one herself; Mrs. Moor very rarely smoked.

For some twenty minutes they talked business. Marshall told them exactly what he had accomplished on the other side, and what still remained to be done.

"Anyhow," said Mrs. Moor, "it seems that the main difficulties have been got over, and the money's quite safe for Isbel?"

"Oh, quite. She may have to wait some months before she can touch it—that's the only thing."

Isbel took little sips of coffee, and looked reflectively into the fire.

"No doubt you'll find a use for it, Isbel, when it does come."

"Oh, it's more sentimental, aunt. Naturally, I don't want to go to Marshall with empty hands."

The others protested simultaneously.

"You needn't cry out," said the girl calmly. "I know it's done everyday, but that's no reason why I should be content to follow suit. After all, why should a married woman be a parasite? It makes her out to be a kind of property. And that's not the worst. . ."

"Very well, child. You've got the money—don't make a fuss."

"Isbel's right, mind you," said Marshall. "There's a decent amount of cold horse-sense about what she says. A girl wants to feel independent. I'm not gifted with a great deal of imagination, but I can see it must be pretty rotten to have to keep on good terms with a man—even when she's not feeling like it—simply and solely for the sake of his cash."

"I wasn't thinking so much of my attitude as yours," replied Isbel.

"Now, that *is* rather uncalled for. It isn't at all likely that a question of private means is going to affect my behaviour. What made you come out with that?"

"Oh, I don't mean it in your sense," said Isbel. "I don't mean anything brutal or tyrannical, of course. I simply say that your whole attitude towards me would be unconsciously modified, and you couldn't help it. Being a man, the mere knowledge that you held the purse would be bound to make you kinder and more chivalrous towards me. That would be a lifelong humiliation. I should never be able to feel quite sure whether you were being kind to me or to my poverty."

"Rot!" exclaimed Marshall. "That sort of thing doesn't exist in married life."

"I couldn't bear to ask for love and be fed with sympathy." Her voice was cold, quiet, and perfectly unembarrassed.

"You girls are all the same," said Mrs. Moor pettishly. "You have that word 'love' on the brain. Most married women are very thankful to have an occasional dish of sympathy set before them, I can assure you. We all know what love *without* sympathy is."

"What?"

"Pure, brutal egotism, my dear. If that's what your heart is crying for, so much the worse for you."

"Perhaps that's what I want, all the same. Every woman has a savage streak in her, they say. I should probably always sell myself to the highest bidder—in love. . . You'd better look out, Marshall."

"Well, it's a lucky thing we both know you as well as we do," said her aunt, dryly.

"The question is, *do* you know me?" Isbel fingered the lace of her corsage.

"The question is, what is there to know? Girls may be exceedingly mysterious to young me, but they're not in the least mysterious to old women, my dear. You've over-indulged in Russian literature lately."

Her niece laughed, as if unwillingly. "If all girls are so hopelessly alike, what becomes of ancestral traits?"

"You don't claim more ancestors than other people, I hope? What is this new pose of inscrutability, child?"

Marshall thought it high time to interrupt the duel, which threatened to develop into something unpleasant.

"To change the subject," he said, rather hastily, "have you got fixed for a house yet, Mrs. Moor?"

"No, I haven't. Why?"

"Would Sussex suit you?"

Isbel anticipated her aunt's reply, turning to him with a friendly smile, as if anxious to counteract the impression caused by her free speaking. "Have you heard of something? Whereabouts in Sussex?"

"Near Steyning."

"You get there from Worthing, don't you?"

"You get there from anywhere, in a car. It's not far from Brighton."

"Tell us all about it. What kind of a house is it?"

"Surely I may speak, Isbel!" said her aunt irritably. "Is it a large property, Marshall? How did you come to hear of it?"

"It's an Elizabethan manor. Two hundred acres of ground go with it, mostly timber. The hall goes back to the thirteenth century. I met the owner coming across."

"And the price?"

"He declined to say off-hand. As a matter of fact, he's not frightfully keen on selling at all. His wife's just died in San Francisco, so I snatched the opportunity and asked him what his plans were about going back. He hasn't decided yet, but I've got a sort of idea that a prompt bid might do the trick, if it at all appeals to you."

"Poor fellow! At least, I hope so. . . Young or old?"

"He told me his age—fifty-eight. He was in the Birmingham brass trade. His name's Judge. You don't know him by any chance?"

"Do we, Isbel?"

"No."

"He is quite a decent chap. He and his wife have lived at Runhill Court for eight years, so it sounds all right."

"Is that the name of the house?"

"Yes. Historical—supposed to be derived from the old Saxon 'rune-hill,' so he says. The runes were engraved letters, intended to keep off the trolls and blendings. I don't suppose that interests you greatly; what's more to the point is that the place is thoroughly up to date, he tells me. He's spent no end on modern improvements—electric lighting, and so forth. . . Well now, do you feel disposed to take it up?"

Mrs. Moor wriggled in her chair, which was a sign of indecision. Isbel emitted clouds of cigarette-smoke, in the manner of women.

"An Elizabethan manor," she remarked reflectively. "Sounds thrilling. Is there a family ghost?"

"Do you want one?"

"In any case, *you* wouldn't have to live there long, child." Her aunt's tone was sharp. "That is, unless you've been altering your programme, you two, behind my back?"

"We're not conspirators, thanks. It's still to be April."

"Then pray leave me to make my own arrangements. When could I go over to the house, Marshall?"

"Anytime, I fancy. Would you care to have Judge's address in town?"

"Please."

He scribbled it on a scrap of paper, and passed it over.

Isbel eyed him thoughtfully. "Aren't you coming with us, Marshall?"

"Really, I wasn't thinking of doing so. Of course, of you'd like me to. . ."

"We should," said Mrs. Moor. "What day would suit you best?"

"There you have me." He hesitated. . . "Well, as we're all here together, what's wrong with tomorrow morning? I could run you over in the car. The country's looking magnificent."

Mrs. Moor consulted the paper in her hand. "But Mr. Judge is in town, you say? How can we get an order to view between now and tomorrow morning?"

"Yes, I see. . . As a matter of fact, I have an order in my pocket."

"But, my dear boy, in that case why did you wish me to go to the trouble of communicating with Mr. Judge?"

"Yes, why did you?" supplemented Isbel, puckering her brow.

"The order's a personal one, you see, and I had no idea I was coming with you."

The girl stared at him in a sort of bewilderment. "Do you mean you intended to go alone, without us?"

"Well, yes. I purposely didn't tell you, because it's more or less a confidential matter, but the fact is Judge wants a private opinion from me with regard to one of the rooms. . ."

"Go on. What sort of opinion? Do you mean he's planning an alteration, or what?"

"Not an alteration exactly, as far as I'm aware. . . I'm very sorry, Isbel, but it's confidential, as I said before. Having passed my word, of course I'm not at liberty to say anything more about it, much as I should like to. . . However, I shall be only too happy to accompany you both."

She slowly passed her palm backward and forward across her skirt, feeling its texture.

"It's very strange, though. So you meant to hide it from us altogether, this mysterious transaction?"

"I meant to keep my word."

"In plain language, you set out a higher value on the regard of this total stranger than on ours? I don't care two pins about the room, or what he proposes to do with it, but I certainly do care that. . ."

"But, my dear girl. . ."

"Why have you done it? It's disquieting. I shan't know *what* you're keeping back now."

Mrs. Moor gazed sternly at her niece. "Do try not to be a fool, Isbel. If Marshall has passed on his word, do you want him to break it? He's perfectly in the right, only, of course, you must try to work up a scene. Just tell us right out, Marshall—would you rather have us with you, or not?"

"I shall be delighted to have you with me. . . 10.30 in the morning—will that suit?"

"Admirably. Well, that's that. Now you can go downstairs, you two. I want to read. I shan't see you again tonight, Marshall. . . Goodnight! . . . Ring for the waiter, please, as you go past. I want these things cleared away."

She remained sitting bolt upright in her chair, waiting for the servant to come and go, when it was her intention, not to read—she had changed her mind at the very moment of expressing it—but to play. These wretched misunderstandings over nothing at all always left her with an unpleasant taste in her mouth, which she could only rid herself of by entering that other world of pure and lofty idealism.

The two younger people walked slowly downstairs, Isbel slightly leading the way.

"Shall we see if we can get a game of billiards?" asked Marshall, in a somewhat subdued voice.

"If you like."

As they passed by the drawing-room the door was wide open; the room was empty.

"Let's come in here," said the girl.

They did so. She shut the door after them; both remained on their feet.

"May I ask," began Isbel, and a spot of colour came into her cheeks, "if it is your intention to keep confidences from me? I wish to know."

"My dear Isbel—"

"Yes or no?" Her tone was quietly menacing. Marshall felt that the shaping of his whole future very likely depended on the next few words addressed by him to this tranquil, dangerous-mannered girl in black.

He reflected before answering.

"Of course, if you put it in that way, Isbel, I mean to keep nothing from you. I gave my word to Judge, it's true, but I quite see that perhaps I had no right to give it. I fully realise that personal secrets vitiate the whole meaning of marriage."

"Then we'll say no more about it. I'm glad. If we held different views on the subject, it would be rather ominous, wouldn't it? . . . But what really is your compact with this man—what does he want you to do exactly? He's quite a stranger, isn't he?"

"Oh, absolutely."

"Then tell me. I shan't talk."

"I know that. In any case, the affair isn't one of national importance. The truth is, this chap Judge once had—or thought he had—a succession of marvellous experiences in one of the rooms at Runhill; an attic on the top storey which rejoices in the name of the East Room. It happened just after he'd moved into the house, eight years ago, and apparently it's been weighing on his mind ever since. For some unknown reason, it pleases him to imagine that I possess an average quantum of common sense, on which account he has invited my assistance in clearing up the mystery. In a soft moment I agreed—and that's all there is to it."

"But I don't understand. Why *you*? What made him fix on *you*?"

"I really can't say. It just resulted from a casual friendly conversation on board ship, coming home. We happened to be discussing the Fourth Dimension, and all that sort of thing."

"What were these marvellous experiences of his, then?"

"A species of delusion, I take it. Every morning, for a week on end, a flight of stairs used to appear to him in that room, leading up out of a blank wall. He avers that he not only saw them, but used to go up them, but he hasn't the vaguest recollection of what took place on top."

"What an extraordinary fancy!"

"Eventually his wife found him out at it—that is, of course *she* saw nothing, but it frightened him off. He had the room locked, and no one has set foot in it from that day to this. Now she's dead, he appears to think there's no longer the same necessity for secrecy."

"Does he *look* mad?"

"Not in the least. Far from it."

"And you actually promised to investigate?"

"My dear girl, what could I do? I couldn't tell the man to his face that he was a lunatic, could I? There was no way out of it. . . It will be an excuse for a run in the car, anyway."

"So you agreed, simply to spare his feelings?"

"We'll put it that way."

"I think it was rather fine of you, Marshall. . . I'm glad you've told me. I must know *all* your affairs. You see that, don't you?"

"Of course I see it."

Having gained her point, she swiftly took him in both arms, and lifted her lips to be kissed. They both laughed. . . Marshall, however, remained uneasy. After they had separated again—for obviously it was no place for love-making—he thoughtfully scrutinised her powdered face, with its steady, indecipherable eyes.

"While we're by ourselves, perhaps you'll tell me, Isbel—what exactly did you mean just now by that remark about selling yourself to the highest bidder in love: were you serious, or pulling my leg?"

"Yes, I must have love," said the girl quietly.

"I don't contest it. But the point is, you seem to regard love as a sort of jam, to be taken in a spoon. There's no such thing as love independent of a person. It appears to be a matter of indifference to you who that person is, so long as he makes it sufficiently sweet for you."

"Don't let's quarrel. I didn't say it to vex you. It isn't sweetness that I want."

"What then?"

Isbel was silent for a moment. She turned half-away from him, feeling the back of her hair with her white, tapering fingers.

"I don't know. . . Love must be stronger than that. . . I mean, one girl might be content with mere placid affection, and another might ask for nothing better than a thick sentimental syrup. It depends on character. My character is tragic, I fancy."

"I hope not." He stood looking rather puzzled. . . "Tell me one thing, Isbel—you're not by any chance finding our engagement. . . *monotonous*, are you?"

"Oh, no."

"Sure?"

"Quite sure. But isn't it a rather extraordinary question?"

Marshall, gazing at her quietly mocking smile, grew suddenly inflamed.

"I suppose you realise in your heart of hearts that you can do what you like with me, and that's why you are so contemptuous. It's a feeble thing to say, but I'd rather go on struggling for your good opinion all my life, Isbel, than be worshipped by any other woman without an effort on my part."

"You will always have my good opinion, if that's all you want."

He flushed up, and took a step towards her. As she awaited him with the same smile, the handle of the door turned noisily from the outside. They started guiltily away from each other.

"Then we'll see if we can get a game of billiards," remarked Isbel in a conversational voice, turning her neck to glance at the two ladies who were entering.

Marshall assented, and they at once left the room.

II

THE VISIT TO RUNHILL COURT

After the breakfast on Saturday morning, Marshall brought the car round. He strolled up and down for sometime, smoking, before the ladies made their appearance in the portico of the hotel. Isbel wore a new travelling-ulster with a smart check; her small, black satin hat was completed by a floating veil. Her face was powdered, and she was rather heavily scented. Mrs. Moor's short, commanding person was dressed with plain dignity. She looked the more distinguished of the two.

Isbel walked round the new car, appraising it critically, Marshall had bought it two months earlier, but delivery had been postponed until his return from America.

"Looks rather ladylike," he apologised, "but it's a devil to go."

Aunt and niece were in the best of humours. The morning was ideal for motoring, while an objective, of course, made it so much more interesting. It was hot, breathless, misty—a typical September day. The sun beat down from a cloudless sky, and the sea was like milk. Crowds of holiday-makers thronged the parade, a piano-organ up some back street was rattling out a popular tune, everyone looked in good health and free from care.

"Can we get back for lunch?" demanded the older lady.

"We'll do our best. It's about fifteen miles each way, I take it."

"Come on, then, and don't waste time."

As Isbel lightly touched Marshall's arm in following her aunt into the back seat, she gave him an intimate smile. Their somewhat dangerous conversation of the preceding evening was forgotten, and both felt the engagement to be a wonderful thing. Climbing in behind the wheel, the underwriter's face took on a deeper colour.

They started. The girl was delighted with the easy running of the car; its power, smoothness, and silence were something impressive. She was voluptuous by nature, and enjoyed luxurious travel, just as she enjoyed every form of softness. Mrs. Moor, for her part, sat as nearly upright as the thickly-padded cushions would permit, staring severely at the throng, which gradually thinned as they approached Hove.

Their road ran through Portslade, Shoreham, and up the valley of the Adur. The sun steadily increased in power, while the morning mists insensibly dissipated. They passed from sunshine to shadow, and from shadow to sunshine, fanned all the time by their own wind. Isbel's first exhilaration faded: she wrinkled her brow, and grew dreamy, pensive, vaguely anxious. Nature always had this effect on her. Streets, ships, crowds, any form of human activity, enabled her to forget herself, but natural surroundings threw her back on her own mental resources, and then the whole emptiness and want of purpose of her life loomed up in front of her. . . Her aunt viewed the changing landscape sternly. These trees, these fields and meads, but, above all, those bare downs of grass-covered chalk in the background, were to her *sacred.* Isbel respected her mood, and made no attempt at conversation.

Presently they came to Bramber and Steyning. At the latter place Marshall slowed down to inquire the way, and was instructed to take the left-hand fork about a mile further on. Runhill Court would be, roughly, three miles north-west from that point, but the road was a complicated one.

The Downs were on their left. Chanctonbury Ring, with its crest of dark trees, dominated the whole country. The sun blazed, while a plague of flies swarmed round the car, which had to crawl as soon as they entered the puzzling network of by-lanes. They met few people, and the way was hard to pick up, in consequence of which it was already nearing twelve when at last they drew up before the lodge gate at their destination.

Beyond the gate a winding carriage drive went forward to the house, which was out of sight; it was bordered on either side by the usual shrubbery of rhododendrons, hollies, etc. on the left, again, was a rising park, containing some fine specimens of beech, while to the right a real wood appeared, the extent of which, however, could not be seen. An ancient, moss-grown, red brick wall bounded the estate. On the other side of the narrow lane which passed the lodge were meadow lands, fringed by a line of tall elms, which effectually shut out the view. It was a solitary and charming spot. The air was peculiarly sweet, clean, yet heavy with fragrance.

As Marshall was in the act of getting down, a middle-aged woman emerged from the lodge. She was smoothing her dress and hair, and evidently had just removed an apron.

He produced Judge's order. The woman took it in her hand and proceeded to read it, passing her thumb under each line from side to side of the sheet, while her lips silently framed the words. She was a tall, big-boned, fresh-complexioned person, of the upper-servant type; handsome, in a common way, but with sarcastic eyes. Her hair was thick and yellow.

Having examined the signature musingly, she turned again to him.

"When did you want to see the house, sir?"

"Now, if we may."

She stared at one of the buttons of his coat. "That makes it rather awkward, sir. I gave the house-key to an American gentleman a short time back, and he's still over there. Will you wait?"

"I didn't know you admitted the general public."

"We don't, sir. This was another order, like yours."

"Someone Mr. Judge picked up on the other side, no doubt. . . Well, Mrs. . ."

"Mrs. Priday, sir."

"Well, Mrs. Priday, I don't see that it matters at all; we shan't interfere with each other. As the house is open, I suppose we can get in?"

"Oh, yes—but did you wish me to show you over?"

"If you will."

"I must find my husband first, before I can leave the lodge. He's working somewhere in the grounds; he's head gardener here. Will the ladies step inside and wait, sir?"

"Well, look here, Mrs. Priday—we're somewhat pressed for time, so if you'll open the gate we'll just run up to the house and be starting. You can follow when you're ready."

"As you please, sir," replied the caretaker, with an almost imperceptible shrug. She proceeded, without any great show of alacrity, to unlatch and swing open the carriage-gate, and meanwhile Marshall returned to the car, which a minute later passed slowly through the entrance to the drive.

Travelling at low speed, they obtained round the first bend, about three hundred yards further on, their first view of the house. It stood on high ground, and cool, dark-green lawns sloped down from it on all four sides. The front, which they approached, faced the south-east. It was a large edifice, in the Elizabethan style, but the exterior had been so renovated and smartened—perhaps by Judge—that it looked almost a modern erection. The irregular, many-gabled roof was bright with new tiles, the facing of red bricks on the ground storey had been pointed recently, while the two upper storeys were plastered with dazzling white stucco.

The house was long-fronted, possessing a double row of lattice windows overlooking the gravel terrace at the head of the lawn. A small, square wing, about thirty feet in height, jutted from the left end of the front, and appeared to belong to a different order of architecture. This was the famous thirteenth-century hall, built during the reign of the first Edward. Its steeply-pointed roof was covered with grey slates. The wide double-door was resplendent with dark green paint and highly polished brass.

Mrs. Moor, as she continued to gaze at it, reflected that the possession of so stylish and picturesque a dwelling would not disgrace her in the eyes of her social circle.

"One might live here very comfortably, Isbel?"

Her niece gave a smile of vexation. "Since you have absolutely determined to immure yourself in the heart of the wilds."

"Pray don't let us thrash that out again," said the old lady. "The suburbs I cannot endure, town flats are prisons, while hotels will be impossible after you've left me. Here, at all events, I should have space and independence."

Isbel turned away without replying.

The car stopped outside the hall porch, with its green door. It was exactly mid-day. The sun glared down, but a refreshing breeze fanned their faces. The house was built on such an elevation that they could see a section of the distant country before them—Adur valley, with the Downs on both flanks, and, right down at its mouth, the sea at Shoreham.

Marshall stamped the ground with his foot. "This must be the original Run Hill that we're standing on."

"Has it a history, then?" asked Isbel.

"Every place must have a history. To me, the mere fact that the ancient Saxons knew it by the same name is rather inspiring."

"Because you're of Saxon blood. I'm a Celt."

"As if that had anything to do with it."

"And then, *Saxons* is a very general term. There were Saxon rustics, and there were Saxon pirates. If you're referring to the latter I might feel sympathetic. It must be awfully jolly to annihilate people you don't like."

"Possibilities, anyhow."

Mrs. Moor became impatient. "Did we come here to discuss your character, Isbel, or to see the house?"

Isbel grimaced in silence, and jerked back once again the veil which kept straying over her shoulder.

Having locked the wheel of the car Marshall walked across to the hall door, and tried the handle. The door opened smoothly and noiselessly. The ladies discarded their wraps, and followed him into the house.

A small lobby brought them to the main hall. Its age, loftiness, and dim light reminded them of an ancient chapel. It was two storeys in height; everything was of wood. The dark-oak, angular roof was crossed by massive beams, the walls were wainscoted, the floor was of polished oak, relieved only by a few Persian rugs, of dignified colours. At the back of the hall, halfway up, a landing, or gallery, ran across its entire breadth. It was reached by a wide staircase, with shallow steps, heavily carpeted, which formed the right-hand exit of the downstairs chamber. Two doors were underneath the gallery, communicating with the interior of the house. A big, ancient fireplace occupied the centre of one of the side walls; against the opposite one stood a modern steam-heating apparatus. Three perpendicular windows over the lobby-door had alternate diamond panes of coloured and uncoloured glass; the colours were dark blue and crimson, and whatever object these rays fell upon was made beautiful and sombre. . . The woodwork was in excellent repair, and appeared newly polished. Al the appointments of the hall were bright, spotless, and in perfect condition. Judge evidently had had the place thoroughly restored and redecorated. And yet the general effect was not quite satisfactory. Somehow, it was *discordant.* . .

Marshall gazed around him with an uncertain air.

"Rather over-modernised, isn't it? I mean, a place like this ought to be more a museum."

"Not at all," said Mrs. Moor. "It's a lounge."

"I know—but would anyone dream of using it as such? Could I smoke a pipe and read a newspaper here? What I say is, why not frankly make a show-place of it?"

"But how? I don't know exactly what you're complaining of."

"Oh, for heaven's sake, don't be so obtuse, aunt!" exclaimed Isbel, irritably. "He merely means, it's all too spick-and-span. When one goes back a few centuries, one expects a certain amount of dust. I quite agree with Marshall. And of course the furniture's hopeless."

"What's wrong with the furniture?"

"Oh, it's a curiosity-shop. All styles and periods. . . Either Mr. Judge has frantic taste or his wife had. Probably the late lamented. I imagine *him* as the sort of man to be ruled entirely by shopmen, and no one can accuse shopmen of being eccentric."

"You're showing off to Marshall," said Mrs. Moor curtly. "Of one thing I'm certain. Mr. Judge must be a highly *moral* man. Order and cleanliness like this could only spring from a thoroughly self-respecting nature."

"If soap and water constitute morality," retorted Isbel.

Time was precious. They passed through the left-hand door beneath the gallery, and found themselves in the dining-room. It was a long, low, narrow, dusky apartment, extending lengthwise from the hall. The noon sunshine filled it with solemn brightness, but the hand of the past was upon everything, and the girl's heart sank as she contemplated the notion of taking her meals here, if only for a few months. She became subdued and silent.

"I fancy you're not impressed?" whispered Marshall.

"It's all so horribly weird."

"I quite understand. You think it would get on your nerves?"

"Oh, I can't express it. It's ghostly, of course—I don't mean that. . . The atmosphere seems *tragical* to me. I should have a constant feeling that somebody or something was all the way waiting to trip me up. I'm sure it's an unlucky house."

"Then you'd better tell your aunt. I suppose you will have the final say in the matter."

"No, wait a bit," said Isbel.

They passed into the kitchens. They were spotless, up-to-date, and fitted with all modern appliances. Mrs. Moor was delighted with all that she saw.

"No expense has been spared here evidently," she spoke out. "So far the house strikes me as eminently satisfactory in every way, and I am very glad you introduced it to my notice, Marshall. If only the rest is equally convenient. . ."

"We're of one mind about this part of it, anyway," said Isbel. "If I'm doomed to live at Runhill this kitchen will be where I shall spend the greater part of my time."

Her aunt gave her a sharp look. "Do you mean you don't like the rest of the house?"

"I'm not infatuated."

"I couldn't stay long in that hall, for example, without reckoning how many coffins had been carried downstairs since it was first built."

"Oh, rubbish, child! People die everywhere."

Isbel said nothing for a minute; then, "I wonder if she were old or young?"

"Who?"

"Mr. Judge's wife."

"Why, what makes you think she might be young?"

"I have a sort of impression that she might be. I haven't succeeded in placing her in this house yet. . . Do you think he'll marry again, Marshall?"

"Judging by the way he avoided women on board I should say not."

Mrs. Moor glanced at her wrist-watch.

"It's getting on towards half-past, and we've two more floors to see yet. We mustn't stand about."

They returned to the hall, and immediately began the ascent of the main staircase. So far they had neither seen nor heard anything of the American visitor; everything in the house remained as still as death. Mrs. Priday, too, was a long time in putting in an appearance. . . The landing, which constituted a part of the hall, was lighted by its windows; the golden sunlight, the black shadows cast by the balustrade, the patches of deep blue and crimson, produced a weird and solemn phantasmagoria of colour. All the air smelt of eld. They stopped for a minute at the top of the stairs, looking down over the rail of the gallery into the hall.

Mrs. Moor was the first to get to business again. She took a rapid survey of their situation. On the left, the gallery came to a stop at the outer wall of the hall. Two doors faced them; one opposite the head of the stairs, the other, which was ajar, further along to the left. On the right, beyond the foot of a second flight of stairs leading upwards, the landing extended forward as a long, dark corridor having rooms on both sides. The obscurity, and a sharp turn, prevented the end from being seen.

Isbel called attention to a plaster nymph, standing in an alcove.

"Mrs. Judge must have put that there," she said, rubbing her forehead; "and I am sure she was little more than a girl."

Her aunt regarded her askance. "What do you know about it?"

"I have a feeling. We'll ask Mrs. Priday when she comes. I think Mr. Judge is a very susceptible elderly gentleman with a *penchant* for young women. Remember my words."

"At least you might have the decency to recollect that you're in his house."

The words were hardly out of Mrs. Moor's mouth when they were startled by a strange sound. It came from the open door on their left, and was exactly like a single chord struck heavily on the piano. They looked at one another.

"Our Transatlantic friend," suggested Marshall.

Mrs. Moor frowned. "It's singular he didn't hear us come in."

Another chord sounded, and then two or three more in quick succession.

"He's going to play," said Isbel.

"Shall I go and investigate?" asked Marshall; but Mrs. Moor held up her hand.

The music had commenced.

The ladies, who possessed a wide experience of orchestral concerts, immediately recognised the Introduction to the opening movement of Beethoven's A major Symphony. It did not take long to realise, however, that the American—if it were the American—was not so much attempting to render this fragment from giant-land, as experimenting with it. his touch was heavy and positive, but he picked out the notes so tardily, he took such liberties with the *tempo*, there were such long silences, that the impression given was that he must be reflecting profoundly upon what he played. . .

Mrs. Moor looked puzzled, but Isbel, after her first shock of surprise, grew interested. She had an intuitive feeling that the unseen performer was not playing for the pleasure of the music, but for someother reason; but what this other reason could be, she could not conceive. . . Could it be that he was a professional musician, who was taking advantage of the presence of a grand piano to go over something in the work which was not quite clear in his mind? Or was the performance suggested by the house?

She knew the composition well, but had never heard it played like that before. The disturbing excitement of its preparations, as if a curtain were about to be drawn up, revealing a new marvellous world. . . It was wonderful. . . most beautiful, really. . . Then, after a few minutes came the famous passage of the gigantic ascending scales, and she immediately had a vision of huge stairs going up. . . And, after that, suddenly *dead silence*. The music had ceased abruptly. . .

She glanced round at her friends. Marshall was lounging over the rail of the gallery, his back to the others; stifling yawn after yawn; her aunt was staring at the half-open door, with an absent frown. The pianist showed no sign of resuming; two minutes passed, and still the deathly silence remained unbroken. Marshall stood erect and grew restive, but her aunt raised her hand for quiet. Isbel silently fingered her hair.

While they still waited, the floor of the room from which the sounds had issued opened to its full extent, and the musician appeared standing on the threshold, tranquilly smoking a newly-lighted cigarette.

III

In the Upstairs Corridor

The stranger was dressed in a summer suit of grey flannel, and dangled a broad-brimmed Panama hat in his hand. Nothing indicated that he had observed their little group.

Mrs. Moor tapped her heel smartly on the floor. He at once looked round, but with perfect self-possession. He was a shortish, heavily-built man, perhaps fifty years of age, having a full, florid face, a dome-like forehead, and a neck short, thick and red—an energetic, intellectual type of person, probably capable of prolonged periods of heavy mental exertion. His head was bald to the crown, the remaining fair was sandy-red and he wore a short, pointed beard of the same colour. His somewhat large, flat, pale blue-grey eyes had that peculiar look of fixity which comes from gazing at one set of objects and thinking of something totally different.

"Are you the American gentleman?" interrogated Mrs. Moor, from a distance. He strolled towards them before replying.

"I do belong to the American nation." His voice was thick, but not unpleasant; it had very little accent.

"They told us you were here, but we were not anticipating a musical treat."

He laughed politely. "I guess my apology will have to be that I forgot my audience, madam. I heard you all come in, but you disappeared somewhere in the house, and the circumstance went clean out of my mind."

Mrs. Moor glanced at the bulky note-book stuffed into his side-pocket, and risked a shrewd conjecture.

"Artists, we know, are notoriously absent-minded."

"Why, I do paint, madam—but I don't put that forward as an excuse for discourtesy."

"Then you were lost in the past, we will say. You have few such interesting memorials in your country?"

"We have some; we are putting on years. But I'm interested in this house in a special sense. My wife's great-grandfather was the former proprietor of it—I don't know just how you call it here. . . well, the *squire*."

Isbel fastened her steady, grey-black eyes on his face. "But why were you playing Beethoven in an empty house?"

The singular, softly-metallic character of her voice seemed to attract his attention, for he shot a questioning glance at her.

"I was working something out," he replied curtly, after a brief hesitation.

"Is it permissible to inquire what?"

He looked still more surprised. "You wish to know that? . . . Some ideas came to me in this house which seemed to require music to illustrate them—that particular music, I mean."

"Do you know Mr. Judge personally?"

"I do not."

Isbel went on gazing at him meditatively, and seemed inclined to pursue the conversation, but at that moment a sound was heard in the hall below. Glancing over the balustrade, they saw Mrs. Priday entering from the lobby.

"I'll have to be going," remarked the American.

No one offered to detain him; the ladies smiled, while Marshall raised his hat. The artist bowed gravely, clapped his own hat on and turned to go downstairs.

In the hall he stopped beside the caretaker for a moment in order to slip a coin into her hand. After that he went out, and the door closed behind him.

"What is the name of that gentleman?" asked Mrs. Moor of the woman, as soon as the latter had joined them.

"Mr. Sherrup, madam."

"Oh! . . . Well, Mrs. Priday, we've now seen the whole of the ground floor, and we're waiting for you to show us over the rest, if you will be so good. And first of all—what are those two doors there?"

"The drawing-room, madam, and what used to be the old library, but Mr. Judge has turned it into a billiard-room. The new library's at the end of the corridor. That's all the sitting-rooms on this floor."

"Very good, then I think we'll first see the drawing-room."

Mrs. Priday without delay ushered them into the apartment in which Sherrup had been playing the piano. It was immediately over the dining-room, and had the same outlook; its windows overlooked the side and back of the house. Quite evidently it was the sanctum of the late lady of the manor—no man could have lived in that room, so full of little feminine fragilities and knick-knacks as it was, so bizarre,

DAVID LINDSAY

so frivolous, so tasteless, yet so pleasing. And underneath everything loomed up the past, persisting in discovering itself, despite the almost passionate efforts to conceal it. . . A chill struck Isbel's heart, and at the same time she wished to laugh.

"Her *taste*!" she exclaimed. "Couldn't she *see* it was all wrong? How old was she, Mrs. Priday?"

"Who, miss?"

"The late Mrs. Judge."

"She was thirty-seven, miss."

"Twenty years younger than her husband. I wasn't so far out, aunt. . . Were they happy together?"

"Why shouldn't they be happy together, miss? Young husbands are not always the kindest."

"What was she like?"

"Small, slight, and fair, miss; pretty and soft-spoken, with a weakish mouth, but the sharpest tongue that ever was."

Mrs. Moor looked annoyed, but Isbel persisted with her questions.

"Did they get about together much?"

"Yes and no, miss. She was one for society, while the master likes no one's company so much as his own. He will shut himself up with a book by the hour together. And then he's fond of long tramps in the countryside; and he belongs to an antiquarian society—they go on excursions and suchlike."

"Did she go with them?"

The caretaker smiled. "She hated them like a swarm of earwigs, miss. She used to call them most terrible names."

"Poor Mrs. Judge!"

"How long have you been in service here?" demanded Mrs. Moor.

"Eighteen years, madam, I married Priday eighteen years ago. He's been here all his life, and his father and grandfather, too. Many people they've seen come in, and many people they've seen go out."

"Most interesting! Has Mr. Judge been down here yet since his return?"

"Not yet, madam. We've had letters, and that's all."

They passed through the billiard-room. Isbel contrived to linger behind with Marshall for a moment.

"Which is the room we have to see?"

"Upstairs. I think I told you it's called the East Room."

"I'm growing more fascinated now. It certainly has an atmosphere of its own, this house. Whether pleasant or unpleasant I can't decide yet."

He pressed her arm. "I sincerely hope you *will* like it, for I don't see how our marriage is going to come off till your aunt gets fixed."

She looked back at him affectionately, but said nothing. Meanwhile Mrs. Moor had followed the caretaker into the corridor, where she awaited them impatiently. They proceeded without loss of time to visit the bedrooms on that floor. Some were large, some were mere boxes, but the appointments of all were modern, hygienic, and expensive. Whoever spent a night at Runhill Court was sure of a luxurious room. The views, too, from the windows were magnificent. Nevertheless the same oppressive sense of antiquity pervaded everything, and once again the same disagreeable doubts sprang up in Isbel's mind.

"It certainly isn't hard to understand how a place like this might affect a man's sanity, if he lived here long enough," she whispered to Marshall. "I am sure I should begin to see things, myself, from the very first night. . . But he must be mad—what do you think?"

"Probably. Should you like to meet him, and judge for yourself?"

"Yes, Marshall!"

"I'll see if I can arrange it."

"Please try. I'm certain he's an extraordinary man, quite apart from the question of hallucinations."

The others by this time were in the library, where the younger couple hastened to join them. Mrs. Moor at once drew Isbel into a corner of the room.

"We've seen practically everything that counts now. How are we to decide?"

"I don't think I could live here, aunt, but don't settle anything in a hurry. You can't imagine what strange thought I have. At one time I feel I hate and loathe the place, and at another—I can't express *what* I feel. There's something very uncanny about it all, and yet it isn't *ghostly*, in that sense. . . There's some living influence. . . I do wish we hadn't parted from Mr. Sherrup so abruptly. I feel positive he could have thrown some light on it."

"Your nerves must be desperately out of order, child, and, that being the case, I strongly doubt whether such a house as this is suitable for you. However, as you say, nothing need be decided on the spur of the moment. . . now we'll see upstairs, and then go home."

It was nearly one o'clock.

The upper landing had a low, sloping roof. It was lighted by a gable window facing the south-west. Opposite to the head of the stairs were

DAVID LINDSAY

two servants' rooms, while on the right hand a passage ran through to the other end of the house, dimly lighted along its entire length by skylights. Doors opened out here and there from both sides; those on the right were dark lumber-rooms, the others were the remaining servants' bedrooms, possessing windows which faced the back of the house. At the far end of the building the servants' staircase came up from the ground floor.

After a cursory walk through, the party returned to the other landing.

"Now, is that all?" demanded Mrs. Moor.

"Yes, madam."

Marshall pinched his chin thoughtfully. "Which is the East Room?"

"It's locked, sir."

"Locked, is it? But Mr. Judge told me he was giving instructions to have it opened."

"I don't know anything about that, sir. It's locked."

"That's unfortunate. At all events, show us where it is."

Mrs. Moor cast him a keen glance, but held her tongue.

"We shall have to go through a rather dark passage, sir—if you don't mind that. It's this way."

Parallel with and overlooking the stairs was another little corridor, stretching to the front of the house and lighted by a dormer-window at the end. Along this Mrs. Priday conducted them. When they could nearly touch the sloping roof, the corridor turned sharply to the left and became a sort of tunnel. Marshall begin to strike matches.

"By Jove, it *is* dark!"

"It gets lighter directly, sir."

After twenty paces or so, there came another twist. A couple of shallow stairs brought them up into a widening of the passage which might almost be described as a room. Its rafters were the interior of a great gable, through the high-set window of which the sun was slanting. Everything had been scrubbed clean, but there was not a stick of furniture.

"The man who designed this house must have had a queer brain," remarked Isbel, with a smile. "Do you mean to tell me that all this leads only to the one room?"

"That's all, miss."

They had paused for a minute to take advantage of the light, before plunging into the next section of night-like corridor. While they stood there, a look of perplexity appeared on Isbel's face, as she seemed to listen to something.

"What's that?" she whispered.

"What?" asked her aunt.

"Can't you hear a sound?"

They all listened.

"What's it like, Isbel?" inquired Marshall.

"Surely you can hear it! . . . a find of low, vibrating hum. . . like a telephone wire while you're waiting for a connection. . ."

But no one else could catch the noise.

"Judge spoke of some sound in a corridor," said Marshall. "He told me everyone couldn't hear it. Kind of a thunder, is it?"

"Yes. . . yes, perhaps. . . It keeps coming and going. . . A low buzz. . ."

"That must be it, then—unless, of course, it's a ringing in your ears."

Isbel uttered a short laugh of annoyance. "Oh, surely I can tell a sound when I hear one? It's exactly as if I were listening on the telephone for an answer to a call. A voice might speak at any moment."

"Foolishness!" said her aunt irritably. "If it's anything at all, it's probably an outside wire of some sort. . . Come along!"

"I can't understand why nobody else hears it. It's so unmistakable."

"Well, nobody else does, child—that's enough. Are you coming, or are you not?"

"It's really quite impressive, though. Like an orchestra heard through a thick wall."

"The question is, are we to stay here until you've succeeded in working yourself up into a fit of enthusiasm over it?"

"I wonder if this is what Mr. Sherrup heard? Very likely it is. It certainly does give one the idea of a *preparation* for something. It's exciting. . . oh, don't glare at me, aunt, as if I were some wild animal—I'm quite in my right senses, I assure you."

"That may be so; but if it's a joke I don't know why you should fix on lunch-time for it. How much longer do you propose to keep us here, may I ask?"

Isbel at last consented to proceed, but there was a strange look in her eyes for all the rest of the time she was upstairs.

The second section of unlighted passage led to another gable-room, and this in turn was succeeded by a third, but shorter, tunnel. Towards the end it was dimly illuminated by a skylight. The passage was terminated by a plain oak door.

DAVID LINDSAY

"Is this the East Room?" asked Marshall.

"Yes, sir."

He tried the handle, but the door was locked.

"Well, that's no go, then!"

"Why is it kept locked?" asked Mrs. Moor.

"Because Mr. Judge wishes it, madam."

They could not tell from Mrs. Priday's expression whether she were being impertinent, or merely simple. Isbel, however, hazarded another question:

"Is the room haunted?"

"Please?"

"I say, is the room haunted?"

The caretaker smiled, as she wrapped her hands in the apron she wore. "If you mean ghosts, miss, I've never heard of any such."

"I'm simply asking of it has the reputation of being queer in anyway?"

"Well, for one thing, miss, it's very old. Priday says it's far and away the oldest part of the house—all this end is. It wouldn't be natural if *no* stories was told about an ancient room like this."

"What kind of stories?"

"Ah, my husband's the one for all that, miss. He'll tell you all you want to know about the house—if you can get him to talk, that is. Not many can. The master never could get much out of him. The Pridays have served here for more than a hundred years, and it's to be expected that my husband knows a goodish bit about the place, which he doesn't want to lose by selling to the first asker. You talk to him, miss, and if he's in the mood he'll tell you some funny stories. I don't pretend to know much about it myself."

"Do you say that this part of the house is older than the hall?" asked Marshall.

"My husband says it's nigh fifteen centuries old, sir, only it's been patched up from time to time, and made to look more like the rest of the house."

"That's rather interesting. I wonder if Judge know it?"

No one answered him. Mrs. Moor again consulted her wrist-watch.

"We really must be getting back—we shall lose our lunch. You'll have to see the room somether time, Marshall, if it's a case of necessity."

There was nothing else to do, and they retraced their steps. Returning through the corridor, they descended the stairs. When once again in the hall, the ladies thanked Mrs. Priday and prepared to go outside, but Marshall stayed behind for a moment to slip a treasury-note in her hand.

Priday himself opened the lodge-gate to allow the car to pass. He was a tough, wrinkled little fellow of about fifty-five, with cheeks like Kentish apples, and a pair of small, wary, twinkling, sloe-black eyes. Isbel viewed him with great curiosity, but no words were exchanged.

"Then we'll run over there again next week-end, providing I can get the key of that room?" asked Marshall of Isbel on the same evening, at the hotel.

She looked at him closely. "Yes. And when you write to Mr. Judge, hint to him that aunt is quite prepared to bid for the house. You know how to put it."

"But is that definite?"

"Certainly. She may not know her own mind, but I know it for her. You'll do that?"

"You'd be prepared to live there yourself for a few months?"

"Yes—for it's such a short time that it makes no difference one way or the other."

And she lifted her hand to her hair with such an air of cold abstraction that Marshall thought she was really bored by the whole affair.

IV

The Legend of Ulf's Tower

The fine weather ran into Sunday. Mrs. Moor went to church in the morning, while Isbel dragged the unwilling Marshall with her to the West Pier to hear music. In honour of his return, she had today for the first time got back into colours, and was wearing a light summer frock, with cerise hat; her pale face was powdered as usual. She was a good deal stared at as they sauntered through the double-row of seated people, which had the effect of irritating her, for she was not feeling in a particularly social humour—she had slept abominably on the previous night.

The band was playing in the pavilion, but the windows were open, and they could hear perfectly well outside. They sank into a couple of deck-chairs which happened to be vacant. An undistinguished valse was just slowing to a finish.

A minute later Isbel nudged her escort; with a significant glance she directed his attention to his neighbour on the other side. It was Sherrup.

"Shall I speak?" he whispered.

"Of course."

Marshall drew reflectively at his cigarette, making no sign until the piece ended. Then he turned to the other good-humouredly.

"Bit warm this morning, Mr. Sherrup?"

The thick, red-bearded American was in the act of wiping his over-heated brow with an ornate handkerchief. He slipped it away, and calmly passed his hand over to the underwriter. The tail of his eye rested for a single instant on Isbel's face, but he did not venture to claim the acquaintanceship.

"You've got my name, I see?"

"The caretaker told us. My own name's Stokes—and this is Miss Loment."

Sherrup rose and bowed.

"Staying long in Brighton?" inquired Marshall.

"No, I'm getting back to London in the morning, en route to Italy."

"You won't be seeing Judge, then? You don't know him personally, I think you said."

"Why, no; I've never met him. My wife wished me to take that house in on my trip, so I wrote him about it, and he was good enough to mail me an order. That's all my connection with Mr. Judge."

"You know he's just back from America?"

"They told me at the house."

Isbel whispered to Marshall to change seats. He obeyed, and she found herself between the two men.

"Still in quest of music, it seems, Mr. Sherrup?"

He laughed. "Oh, well, music was invented for lonely men."

"Your wife isn't with you, then?"

"You mustn't blame me for that, Miss Loment. It wasn't my fault. She just wouldn't come. Scared of the sea."

"Is it a professional trip for you, or a holiday?"

"Oh, I'm seeing the galleries, that's all."

"What is your particular branch of art?"

"I'm a portrait-painter."

"How awfully interesting! But don't you have to accept commissions from all sorts of objectionable types?"

"There are no objectionable types, Miss Loment. In an art sense, every man and woman alive is an individual problem, with special features you won't find elsewhere."

"I never looked at it in that light. It must be so. But how absorbing you must find it all!"

Marshall got up.

"I'm going to hunt for cigarettes, if you'll both excuse me. Stay here, Isbel. I won't be long."

"No, don't be long." She turned again to Sherrup.

"Do you find you get most of your applications from women or men?"

"The sexes are about equally vain, Miss Loment; but maybe the ladies are ahead in self-enthusiasm. I couldn't supply the statistics off-hand."

She laughed. A light entr'acte struck up, and further conversation was postponed for a few minutes. Isbel began to tap the pier flooring with the tip of her sunshade nervously and absently. As the last notes sounded she threw a hurried glance to the right, to see if Marshall were returning, and then leant over, almost confidentially, towards her companion.

"Tell me—what did you really think of that house yesterday?"

"A real impressive old pile, Miss Loment."

"Nothing more?"

He gave her a guarded look. "I guess a house can't be much more than a house."

"What made you sit down to that piano, then?"

"Oh, *that*!" He removed his hat, and slowly passed his hand over his broad, prominent forehead. . . "My little performance has surely struck your imagination. I thought we were through with that yesterday."

"But it was a strange notion, you must admit."

"Perhaps I'm a strange character, Miss Loment."

"Don't let's fence. Mr. Stokes will be back directly. I want to know, please—what had the house to do with it?"

Sherrup hesitated. "I had some sensations."

"I thought so. And where did you have them? Wasn't it in the gable of that dark corridor on the top floor?"

There was a short pause.

"We look to be in the same boat, Miss Loment."

"Then it *was* there?"

"Not there, but near there. It was outside the door of that room they call the East Room these days. It used to be Ulf's Tower. Did you get as far?"

"Yes. And what was it you heard?"

"Heard? . . . Oh, I guess you're referring to the sound in that passage? No, it wasn't that, Miss Loment."

"Then what was it? Tell me what happened?" She spoke quickly.

"Nothing *happened*. We were talking of *sensations*, weren't we? . . . I'm an artist, Miss Loment, and that means a bundle of live nerves. My mind gets troubled maybe ten or twenty times a day, without my ever guessing what for. This one was what you might call a bad 'seismic disturbance,' and there's no more to it."

"Perhaps you think my questions are prompted by inquisitiveness? It isn't that. My aunt may be buying Runhill Court, and, if she does, I shall have to live there; so you see my interest is quite legitimate."

Sherrup watched her professionally. The quivering nostrils, the nervous mouth, the peculiar expression of the grey-black eyes, fascinated without satisfying him. Her character possessed an important quality which he was unable to locate on her features. It was contained only in that quiet, pleasant, yet metallic and foreign-toned voice.

"I can't tell you much," he said at length, and then there was another silence.

Isbel glanced around her rather guiltily. "Still, I feel you can tell me something. Can't we talk it over together, somewhere? Obviously it's out of the question here." She laughed, without conviction. "I know it sounds terribly melodramatic, still you understand my point of view, don't you?"

"I shall feel honoured and delighted. But you'll sure be disappointed when you see how little I have to hand over, Miss Loment. . . and another thing—I'm away tomorrow morning, as I told your friend."

"By what train?"

"Eleven A.M."

She pondered. Marshall would depart for town three hours earlier than that.

"Let us fix up something. Can you be outside the turnstiles of this pier tomorrow morning at ten o'clock sharp? That would allow you ample time to catch your train."

"Right. Ten sharp. I'll be there."

"I rely on you, mind."

"Oh, I keep my appointments, Miss Loment," said the American.

Isbel was about to say something else, when turning her eyes, she observed Marshall approaching. During his absence his chair had been appropriated by a pale, stout, flabby lady of uncertain age, with a drooping mouth, and eyes which positively snapped; the usurpation had passed unnoticed by the others.

Sherrup rose. "I'll quit. You take my seat, Mr. Stokes—I'll have a turn along the front till luncheon."

Next morning Isbel breakfasted early with Marshall, and saw him depart for the station. As he intended returning to Brighton for the following week-end, the car and the major portion of his belongings were left behind.

At ten o'clock she was outside the West Pier, Sherrup, who already waited there, immediately came up to her, raising his hat and removing the cigar from his mouth.

"Let's walk towards Hove," she suggested. "It's less crowded that way."

He assented in dry silence.

"It was most kind of you to come out of your way for me," began Isbel. "After all, we are total strangers."

"Now, don't say that; I feel as if I'd known you quite a long time. . . My cigar doesn't worry you any?"

"No, please. . ."

"All right. Now let's get to business. Time's short, Miss Loment. Well, now I'm here for, I conclude, is to specify my sensations at Runhill on Saturday. There wasn't anything else, was there?"

"It won't embarrass you?"

"Oh well, I'm not easily embarrassed. . . Now, I told you where it all happened. Outside the door of that East Room. Honestly, that was one of the things I came to see. I could have just kicked myself when I found that lock fast."

"First of all—you did hear the sound in that corridor, didn't you? My friends didn't—that's why I ask."

"Yes, I heard it. like the far-away scrape of a double-bass."

"Yes, yes—it *was* like that. I couldn't identify the sound it reminded me of, but that was it."

"It's tough to explain, but it might be in the nature of a flow from that East Room to another part of the house."

"Caused by what?"

"I can't say. But is that what was troubling you?"

"It was so horribly uncanny. I can almost hear it still."

"Anyway, we'll quit that, and come to my experience. It isn't a mile long. While I stood outside that door, just after trying to burgle the lock—for I had my knife out to it—a kind of *smell* came wafting over me of a sudden. . . Now, I don't want you to smile, Miss Loment. There needn't be anything funny in a smell. I know, and you know, that a smell can be the powerfullest variety of sensation, when it sets out to be. You can't kill a man by a sight or a sound, but I wouldn't like to say you couldn't kill him with some smells, and not always disagreeable ones at that. That just shows the superior sensitiveness of the nose as an organ. I would like for somebody to take that up as an art. . . Well, this particular odour was of the delirious species. It was like the epitome of a spring day in the woods—all the scent of the pines, and the violets, and the rich, moist, dark brown soil, and whatever else comes carried to you by the breezes—only, all double-distilled, as if it was the spillings of a bottle of a new sort of women's perfume. . ."

"And then?"

"Call to mind where I smelt it all, Miss Loment. In a dark, dusty, airless corridor of an ancient house, which god's air hasn't blown through for centuries. . . I *jumped*—nearly. Then it passed away quite suddenly again. I figure it didn't last all told more than ten seconds. But after it was gone I stood there kind of transfigured, like a man that has just seen a vision. It wasn't till it quitted that I saw its importance. It was like a waft from another world. . . that house is *alive*, Miss Loment."

"Is that the whole?"

"That's all."

"It's very, very strange. But still I don't quite see why it should have suggested that music to you?"

"Yes, now, why did it? But somehow it did. I can't explain it to myself. The suggestion thought has gone, and I can't recover it. . . The orchestra was *tuning up*. Something big was going to happen. Something like that. You mustn't press the resemblance too close. Any kind of big symphonic music might have done, but I just chose that—it must have seemed more appropriate."

Isbel tried unsuccessfully to put indifference into her voice as she asked the question:

"I'm going to make what you may consider a very singular inquiry, Mr. Sherrup. Was your reason for playing that music the fact that the passage of the ascending scales suggested to you the idea of a mysterious gigantic staircase?"

He blew out a cloud of smoke, at the same time looking at her from the corner of his eye.

"Why should that be?"

"I don't know why it should be, or why it should not be; but was it so?"

"It was not. You appear to know something I don't, Miss Loment. What staircase?"

"Oh, nothing. It was just a foolish question. . . Shall we turn back?"

They did so.

Isbel nervously cast in her mind for a change of conversation.

"You say that room used to go by another name. How was that?"

"It was called Ulf's Tower. The story is that Ulf was the original builder of the house. He lived about a hundred years after the first landing of the South Saxons. Four or five houses have been put up on the same site since then, but the name struggled through till a couple centuries ago. My wife's ancestor, Michael Bourdon, set it all down in his papers. The history of Runhill Court goes back to the sixth century Anno Domini."

"But why should that particular room have been selected to preserve his memory?"

"Oh, well, because the missing rooms of the legend were supposed to be immediately above that side of the house. That's quite clear."

"I have heard no legend. What missing rooms?"

"You surely surprise me. I guessed every man, woman, and child in the Old Country would know about the lost rooms of Runhill Court. When Ulf built his house, Miss Loment, it was on haunted land. Run Hill was a waste elevation, inhabited by trolls—which, I figure, were a variety of malevolent land-sprites. Ulf didn't care, though he *was* a pagan. He built his house. I gather he was a tough fellow, away above the superstitions of his time and country. And—well, one day Ulf disappears and a part of his house with him. Some of the top rooms of the Tower were clean carried off by the trolls; it happened to be the east end of the house, the nearest to their happy hunting-grounds. That was the very last that was heard of Ulf, but all through the centuries folks have been jumping up to announce that they've caught sight of the lost rooms. . . That's the fable."

They walked along in silence.

"Then would you advise me to live in that house?" asked Isbel suddenly, with an unsteady smile.

Sherrup smoked for quite a minute before answering.

"If you ask that, Miss Loment, you must have a reason for asking it. tell me what you feel."

"Confessions are so awkward, and I'm not sure you won't laugh."

"I won't laugh."

"Well, then—when I was listening to that weird sound in that passage, it suddenly seemed to strike a very deep string in my heart, which had never been struck before. It was a kind of *passion*. . . It *was* passion. But there was something else in it besides joy—my heart felt sick and tormented, and there was a horrible sinking sensation of despair. But the delight was there all the time, and was the strongest. . . It only lasted a very short time, but I don't think I could ever forget it. . ."

"Yes, I know," said Sherrup.

"Then tell me what it means, and what I'm to do."

He threw away his cigar.

"Do nothing, Miss Loment, and ask no questions. That's the advice of a man who has daughters of his own."

"Not live there, you mean?"

"No." He made an emphatic side-gesture with his hand. "Cut it right out. A house like that is going to do you no good. Shall I tell you what you are, Miss Loment? You're an artist without a profession. You're like a lightning-rod without an outlet—you want to steer clear of all kinds of storms. Oh, I'm not a portrait-painter for nothing. Your nervous system is shining through all right. . . Well, you asked me for it, so I've handed it out. But honestly, I wouldn't take on that house. If you feel like that at the beginning, what are you going to feel after a while? It's too risky?"

"Thank you," she said quietly. "I think I *will* take your advice. I'm afraid I'm rather highly strung by nature, although, oddly enough, not one of my friends appears to have any suspicion of the fact. I pass for being stolid, rather than otherwise. You are almost the first to give me credit for exceptional feelings."

When they had arrived opposite the pier once more, Sherrup took his departure.

So strong was the impression made upon him by Isbel's personality that in the train, before it started, he was induced to commit her elusive features to one of the pages of his precious sketch-book. When it was completed, however, he shook his head with an air of profound dissatisfaction. It was a good likeness, but he still couldn't get that *voice* into the picture.

V

ISBEL SEES HERSELF

M arshall came down again by train on Friday evening. Judge had replied to him during the week, notifying that he was still considering the question of parting with his house, but hoped before long to come to a definite decision. Meanwhile, no useful purpose would appear to be served by a personal interview with the lady desiring to purchase, but he was willing to undertake to give her the first refusal of the estate. He enclosed the key of the East Room. Marshall communicated only the business part of the letter to Mrs. Moor.

The fine weather continuing, he took the ladies on Saturday for a long run through Sussex and Kent. They wound up with the theatre at night.

On Sunday morning, at the breakfast-table, Isbel announced to her aunt the intention of herself and Marshall to motor over to Runhill Court before lunch. Mrs. Moor, although a rigid churchgoer, manifested neither pleasure not displeasure.

"But you *will* be back for lunch this time?"

"Oh, yes. Marshall merely wants to carry out his commission."

"I know you don't like the house, so I needn't warn you against prematurely falling in love with it. I've got a strong feeling he won't part with it."

"Why not?" asked Marshall.

"Oh, I've had some experience of these heart-broken old widowers. He's far more likely to pick up another wife than to renounce an old, familiar home. At his time of life he's not so much a man as a bundle of habits."

"Fifty-eight's not so old."

"Too old for a new establishment, but not too old for a new wife," repeated Mrs. Moor with a shade of contempt.

Her niece reached for the marmalade dish. "I expect there are women who would marry him. He must be decently well off."

"Of course—and even quite young girls. If it's beauty he wants he'll find a wife easier to get than a good cook. Mark my words—within twelve months a second Mrs. Judge will be installed in that house."

"I thought you were an admirer of his," said Isbel nonchalantly.

"I admire his thoroughness in practical matters, but that doesn't blind my eyes to probabilities."

"In other words, you think he's treating you badly by keeping you on tenterhooks. Own up, aunt!"

"You're quite mistaken, child. I'm not attacking him. I'm simply finding reasons for his not being able to make up his mind. It's his own house, and he can do what he likes with it." . . . However, it was obvious that Mrs. Moor was annoyed.

The two younger people left Brighton soon after ten o'clock, and as the road was now more familiar they reached Runhill Lodge almost upon the stroke of eleven. Mrs. Priday did not appear; this time it was her husband who attended the gate. He wore a black coat, in honour of the day, and was smoking a nicotine-stained wooden pipe carved in the likeness of a man's head. Marshall showed him a corner of Judge's letter, with the signature, following it up with a small *pourboire*, which the head gardener thrust indifferently into his pocket.

"Can we get into the house now?"

"Yes, sir."

"Are you at liberty?"

Priday answered in the affirmative.

"As a matter of fact, it's only one room we have to see. We went over all the rest last time. The East Room. It was locked when we were here before, but I've got the key since."

The gardener gazed at him with his cunning eyes for a moment, and then asked cautiously, as if feeling his way: "Now, why would the boss be having that room opened, sir?"

"Any particular reason why it shouldn't be opened?"

"It's been kept locked up for eight years, sir, and that's one good reason."

"Why?" demanded Isbel.

"Oh, there's nothing there for nobody."

"Then why waste a good lock?" . . . Finding that Priday did not reply, she proceeded, "I understand its real name is Ulf's Tower?"

"What name?"

"Ulf's Tower."

"I never heard that, miss. In my grandfather's time, the old 'uns used to call it the elves' Tower."

"How extraordinary! I wonder which version is the right one?"

"Well, we can be talking about all this when we get to the house," said Marshall, "if you'll get the key and let us through."

While Priday went into the lodge Isbel closed her eyes and pressed her hand to her forehead.

"I'm afraid I've a headache coming on."

"Is it the sun? If so, the sooner we get inside, the better."

"It must be the hot sun."

The gardener reappeared almost immediately with the key in his hand, and at once set about opening the carriage-gate. Marshall got back into the car—Isbel had not alighted—they passed through, the gate was closed behind them, and Priday having been invited to mount, they ran smoothly up the drive, and within a minute or two were outside the house.

As they stood waiting by the door, while Priday fumbled with the lock, the throbbing of Isbel's temples grew so unendurable that she hardly knew how to remain erect.

"Worse?" inquired Marshall, with some anxiety.

"I'm afraid so. I wish he'd hurry up."

At the same moment that she spoke, the door was got open, and Marshall supported her into the cool of the hall, where she sat down. The two men remained standing beside her.

"This is better, but I fear I can't go on for a minute or two." . . . After a pause, she addressed Priday more conversationally: "So you know nothing about the East Room?"

"There's no 'so' about it," was the blunt, though not offensive reply. "I never said I didn't."

"But you say there's nothing there?"

"There ain't nothing there that *you* want, miss."

"What do I want?"

"You've come on a picnic, like. . . This house ain't going to be played with. P'raps it'll bite back, and bite hard."

This language, which would have sounded imbecile in another place, seemed almost like a threat to Isbel in their present situation, surrounded as they were by the solemn, silent remains of an extreme antiquity. She discontinued her questions. Marshall, however, who preserved his common sense, took up the story.

"What exactly do you mean by that, Priday?"

"Gentleman like you, sir, can go anywhere about the house. You'll see or hear nothing, and it won't hurt you. Young female nerves is a very different matter. P'raps those who start a funny journey can't always come back when they like. . . The young lady's got a headache, you say. That's a good enough excuse. Let her rest here, sir, while you and me go up to see what you want to see."

"Oh, rot! . . . You want to come, don't you, Isbel?"

"Very much. But really, I'm physically incapable of moving. My head gets worse instead of better."

"Then, shall I stop with you, or would you like me to get the job over? I could be up and down again in ten minutes. Say what you'd like."

"Yes, please go. Take Mr. Priday with you. I think complete silence and solitude may do me good. Talking makes it worse."

"I wish to heaven I could do something for you! . . . You're sure you don't mind being left?"

She gave a feeble, reassuring smile. "Good gracious! I'm not a child."

Marshall took his departure reluctantly upstairs, accompanied by Priday, whose legs, however, stiffened by a lifetime of digging, were soon unable to keep pace with those of the young underwriter.

Isbel now kept shutting and reopening her eyes. The repose, silence, and gloom began to exercise a soothing effect on her nerves, and she had not sat there two minutes before her head became easier. Everything in the hall was as it had been on the occasion of their previous visit. The dark, dignified, polished woodwork was solemnly illuminated as before, by the golden, blue and crimson rays from the mediaeval windows, and there was the same deathly stillness.

Suddenly it occurred to her that she was looking at something the existence of which she had never yet realised. It was a part of the structure of the hall, and she must certainly have seen it before, but, if so, it had completely escaped her observation. It was a second flight of uncarpeted stairs, leading upwards out of the hall, by the side of the ancient fireplace. It did not strike her that there was anything odd about these stairs; they were quite prosaic and real; the only curious circumstance was that hitherto she should have overlooked them in so miraculous a manner.

They went straight forward and up through an aperture in the wall. About a dozen steps were visible, but the top was out of sight. It immediately flashed across her mind that by ascending them she would set foot in a heretofore unexplored part of the house. In the excitement of the discovery she forgot her headache. She got up, stood for a moment in doubt, wondering whether she should call out to

Marshall, and then, deciding that her voice would not carry so far, and that it would be time enough to acquaint him with her find on his reappearance, she resolved in the meantime to do a little pioneering on her own account. Not once did it enter her brain to identify these stairs with those of Judge. They appeared in a different quarter of the house, and, moreover, were too solid and tangible to conjure up the faintest suspicion of anything supernatural. She was not in the least alarmed; merely intensely surprised and curious.

Deliberately, but with a slightly agitated pulse, she ascended the steps one by one, occasionally turning to look back down at the hall. Something in the whole proceeding occurred to her as mysterious, though she was unable to explain to herself just what it was. The steps were of a dark, shining wood, which resembled teak; there were, from bottom to top, seventeen of them. There was no handrail, but the walls enclosed the well of the staircase on either side.

At the head of the flight she found herself standing in a little room, about fifteen feet square, empty of furniture, and lighted from above, although no skylight was visible. The floor, walls, and ceiling were of the same dark, handsome wood as the staircase. It was a kind of ante-chamber. There was nothing to see there, and nowhere to sit down, but there were doors leading out of it. There were three of them; one in the centre of each of the three walls, the head of the stairs occupying the centre of the fourth. All were of plain, undecorated wood, investing them with an almost primitive air. All three were closed.

Isbel hesitated. She wished to proceed, but those closed doors seemed to hold a sort of menace. She now remembered that Mrs. Priday had omitted to show these rooms with the rest of the house—or was it that she had thought they had already seen them prior to her arrival? Or, again, like the East Room, they might be locked; they, too, might contain undesirable mysteries. . . On *that* point, of course, she would satisfy herself at once. . . if it were really possible to go any further. . .

Could it have been something of the same feeling that leads a woman to scrutinise an envelope addressed in an unfamiliar handwriting for several moments before opening it, which induced Isbel to pause for so long outside those doors? It was naturally absurd to suppose that she was actually frightened—so she told herself—and yet, somehow, she could not bring herself to adopt the sensible plan of peeping in. . . The fact was, there was something not quite *right* about them. They were unlike other doors. And not only were they unlike other doors, they were unlike each other. In that fact, perhaps, consisted their chief strangeness. The door in the middle, which she faced, looked noble, stately, and private, whereas the right-hand one had—she could not describe it to herself—a dangerous, waiting appearance, as though the room it belonged to were inhabited and the door at any moment might be flung suddenly open. As for that on the left, most likely it opened on to a passage-way—that was the impression it gave her. . . Perhaps all this hypersensitiveness on her part had its origin in the mutual position of the walls.

For some minutes she was incapable either of impelling herself forward or dragging herself away. She remained standing in nervous embarrassment, biting her gloved fingertips, and smiling at her own weakness. Perhaps she ought to descend again to the hall and wait for Marshall. He might have returned by this time, and be wondering what had become of her. . . It was most extraordinary that he, too, hadn't noticed these stairs! . . .

Unable to muster sufficient courage to attack any of the doors unsupported, she at last determined to return for his assistance. But she had made no allowance for *whim*. While her foot was still on the second stair from the top, she turned straight round, then walked with a springing action across the room to the left-hand door, and, defiantly flinging it wide open, stood on the threshold, staring in with startled eyes.

The room was even smaller than that outside. Its fittings were all of the same dark wood. There was no furniture, but a large oval mirror hung on one of the walls, and on the side of the room furthest from the door, was a long, rich-red curtain, which seemed to conceal another door. Isbel took a tentative step forward. She kept asking herself what these rooms could be for, to what part of the house they belonged, and why they had been left unfurnished.

Abstractedly she walked over to the mirror to adjust her hat. . . Either the glass was flattering her, or something had happened to make her look different; she was quite startled by her image. It was not so much that she appeared more beautiful as that her face had acquired another character. Its expression was deep, stern, lowering, yet everything was softened and made alluring by the pervading presence of sexual sweetness. The face struck a note of deep, underlying passion, but a passion which was still asleep. . . It thrilled and excited her, it was even a little awful to think that this was herself, and still she knew that it was *true*. She really possessed this tragic nature. She was not like other girls—other *English* girls. Her soul did not swim on the surface, but groped its way blindly miles underneath the water. . . But how did the glass come to reflect this secret? And what was the meaning of this look of enchanting sexuality, which nearly tormented herself? . . .

She spent a long time gazing at the image, but without either changing the position of her head, or moving a muscle of her countenance. Petty, womanish vanity had no share in her scrutiny. She did not wish to admire, she wished to understand herself. It seemed to her that no woman possessing such a strong, terrible sweetness and intensity of character could avoid accepting an uncommon, and possibly fearful, destiny. A flood of the strangest emotions slowly rose to her head. . .

She heard a man's voice calling her name from a very long way off. The voice was muffled, as if by intervening walls, but she had no difficulty recognising it as Marshall's. She guessed that he was shouting down from the top of the house, and that, on getting no response, he would quicken his descent to the hall. She would have to go and meet him. Before retracing her steps, however, it was of course essential to peep behind the curtain.

Hastening across to it, she pulled aside the heavy red drapery. There was revealed a doorway, but no door; another flight of wooden stairs started to go down immediately beyond. Isbel persuaded herself that she would still have time to explore a little.

Halfway down, the hall came in sight. . . She could not understand. . .

Near the bottom she realised that she was coming out by the side of the fireplace—in other words, that this staircase was identical with that by which she had ascended. . . How this could possibly be, however, she had no more opportunity of asking herself, for at that moment she reached the hall, and at the very instant that her foot touched the floor every detail of her little adventure flashed out of her mind, like the extinguishing of a candle.

She remembered having commenced the ascent of those stairs, she was perfectly conscious that the ascent of those stairs, she was perfectly conscious that she had that very minute come down them, but of all that had happened to her in the interim she had no recollection whatever.

She turned round to look at the staircase again. It had vanished! . . . It was then, for the first time, that she recalled Mr. Judge's story.

Instinct informed her that the whole transaction must be concealed from Marshall. She required time to think it over quietly and tranquilly, in all its bearings, before taking him into her confidence—if, indeed, she should ever decide to do so. He was very unlikely to put a charitable construction on her tale; it would almost certainly cause disagreement and general unpleasantness—it would be far better never to say anything about it at all. She sat down and waited for him. Her headache had returned.

Presently Marshall, followed by Priday, entered the hall, but not from upstairs—from outside. He appeared rather distracted, and on catching sight of Isbel his face flushed up.

"Where in the name of wonder have you been all this time?"

"All which time? What is the time?"

"It's well past twelve. I've been looking for you a good twenty minutes."

"Oh! . . ."

"Where were you?"

She forced a smile, while thinking rapidly.

"Evidently I wasn't here, since you didn't see me. . . As a matter of fact, I went outside for a few minutes."

Priday regarded her with a dubious stare.

"Even so, you must have heard me shouting," said Marshall.

"My dear Marshall, are you trying to be unpleasant, or what? If I had heard you, I should have answered. Perhaps I dropped off to sleep—I can't say. My head was bad, and I was sitting under some trees, with my eyes closed. I really don't think that you need make such a fuss about it. . . Did you see the room?"

"Of course we saw it. It's just a room like any other room."

"Nothing mysterious?"

"Oh, that's all bunkum! . . . Well are you fit, or would you like to wait a bit longer?"

She got up slowly. "We'd better go."

Marshall looked at her strangely, but said nothing more. They left the house. Marshall went across to the car, but Isbel stopped for a minute to address Priday, who was engaged in locking the door.

"So I should have run no great risk in that room, after all, Mr. Priday?"

He finished his task before looking up or replying.

"That may be, miss—but I ain't taking nothing back. And what's more, I ain't so sure you ain't seen too much, as it is."

"Really, this is most uncalled-for!" she exclaimed, laughing. "Why, what do you imagine I've seen?"

"You know and I don't, miss. All I say is, I see a difference in you since forty minutes ago."

"An improvement, I hope, Mr. Priday?"

"You're amusin' yourself with me, miss—and that's all right. But I ain't one to speak of what I don't know, and I sticks to it—and you mark my words—this house ain't one for young ladies like yourself. There's plenty more old houses in the kingdom for you to see over, if you want such."

"Come along, Isbel!" called out Marshall impatiently from the car. "Don't stand gassing there, with your bad head."

As she obeyed and took her seat, the smile dropped from her face, leaving it so puckered and anxious-looking that he uttered an involuntary exclamation:

"By Jove! You *do* look washed-out."

Isbel made no reply, but after they had repassed through the lodge-gate she unobtrusively produced a small mirror of polished silver from her handbag and carefully scrutinized her features. She certainly was *not* looking very attractive, but otherwise she could detect no special change in her appearance.

VI

Judge Appears on the Scene

It was Tuesday afternoon. Marshall had returned to town. The weather had suddenly broken, and rain had fallen steadily since early morning. Mrs. Moor was in her room, while Isbel, rather reluctantly, took the opportunity of bringing her correspondence up to date—a task she cordially detested. Half a dozen laconic epistles, sealed and addressed in her large, sprawling handwriting, already lay piled on the table, and now she was writing to Blanche, expressing her pleasure at the intimation that she and Roger proposed to spend the coming week-end at the Gondy. Blanche was her old school chum and dearest friend. It was she who had introduced her to Marshall (her husband Roger's younger brother); consequently, she regarded the engagement as her own peculiar handiwork, though of course Isbel held different ideas on the subject, which she kept strictly to herself. Isbel, who was "Isbel" to all the rest of her circle, was "Billy" to Blanche and her husband. They lived at Hampstead, and were fairly well off.

A knock sounded at the door, and a visiting-card for Mrs. Moor was handed in by the hotel hall-boy. Isbel read the name in silent astonishment. Directing the boy to wait, she at once went to her aunt's room.

"Mr. Judge is here," she announced dryly, standing by the door.

The older lady half got up, then lay down again.

"Where is he?"

"Downstairs, presumably. Will you see him?"

"Really, it's most unreasonable! He appears to imagine he's privileged to do whatever he pleases. What an impossible hour to call! . . . Well, I shan't see him, that's all."

"You'd better ascertain what he wants, hadn't you? Shall *I* go down?"

"You? Certainly not, child. Just send down word that I'm not at home, and if he has anything to say he can write."

Isbel smiled remonstratingly. "I think perhaps I'd better go down."

"A pity you're not always so considerate."

"It's only common courtesy, after all. The poor man may have come to Brighton specially."

"Do as you please about it—only, bind me to nothing."

"Don't be absurd, aunt! How can I bind you?"

She went away. Mrs. Moor stared thoughtfully at the closed door, rubbed her eyes, and took up her book again.

"Where is the gentleman?" demanded Isbel of the hall-boy.

"In the lounge, madam."

She accompanied him downstairs. It was not yet the tea-hour and the lounge was nearly deserted. Judge was sitting in a stiff attitude on a straight-backed chair near the door. Although his garments were suited to the weather, he looked exceedingly well-groomed, and Isbel, contrary to her anticipation, was favourably struck. He appeared considerably younger than his reported age, was short, wiry, and clean-looking, and altogether was a thoroughly good and dignified type of wealthy provincial Englishman. His clean-shaven face was sallowish; it possessed power and resolution, quite evidently derived from long practice in handling men. The eyes were grey, shrewd, and steady, and he wore no glasses. . . The boy briefly introduced him, and disappeared.

Judge rose and bowed gravely, waiting for her to speak first.

"Mrs. Moor unfortunately is engaged. I am her niece."

He bowed again. "May I ask your name?"

"I am Miss Loment."

He scrutinised her person somewhat closely. Her rather full bosom was strongly suggested beneath her loose silk afternoon jumper. Her neck was bare. A long chain of amethyst beads hung from it as far as the waist, and with this chain she toyed all the time they stood talking.

"I happened to be in Brighton on other business," he explained, in a pleasant, solemn voice, "and thought to kill two birds with one stone. I'm sorry I've been unlucky. Perhaps you'll be kind enough to convey a message?"

"Of course; I shall be most pleased to."

"You may possibly be aware that Mrs. Moor and I have been in indirect communication, through Mr. Stokes, regarding the sale of my property, Runhill Court?"

"Naturally, I am aware. My aunt and I live together, and always have done."

"Of course, I was ignorant of that. . . Well, Miss Loment, I am sorry to have kept her waiting so long, but at least I've been able to come to a decision. After a very full consideration of the matter and looking at it from all sides, I find it will not be—for the present, at all events—quite advisable to dispose of the estate. I shall confirm it in writing when I get back home, but in the meantime no doubt you will intimate my decision to Mrs. Moor?"

A red blotch appeared suddenly in the centre of each of Isbel's cheeks. . . There was quite a long pause.

"But this decision appears to me very strange," she said at length, in a scarcely audible voice.

"In what respect?"

She lost her head. "I understood from Mr. Stokes that you were anxious to sell your house."

"Mr. Stokes was not authorised by me to make any such statement," replied Judge, in a tone of extreme annoyance. "I have never at anytime expressed anxiety to sell. It was he who suggested the business, and I made my reluctance clear from the very first. There is no breach of faith in any shape or form."

There was a settee situated in a retired corner of the room, and towards this she steered him, without protest on his part. They seated themselves. Isbel smoothed out her skirt and kept throwing nervous glances about her, as though at a loss how to reopen the subject.

"Would it be rude to ask you *why*—I mean. . ." She broke off in confusion.

"Why I don't wish to sell? Because my future movements are uncertain, Miss Loment. There are substantial reasons against my taking up residence there again at the moment, but later on I may wish to do so."

"I see."

There was another awkward silence, the end of which was marked by a bitter smile on Isbel's face.

"No doubt you are more accustomed to dealing with business men, Mr. Judge?"

"Now, what makes you say that?"

"This decision of yours is so blunt. It's almost like a challenge."

"A challenge?"

"I feel just as though I had received a slap on the face."

He fidgeted in his place. "I may have expressed myself rather abruptly, but that was because I had no idea that the matter was of any great importance to you ladies. If I have unwittingly been the means of upsetting your plans, I can only say I am very sorry."

"But you remain stubborn?"

"My dear lady, you hardly realise what you are asking. I have lived in that house for eight years, and it is associated with the happiest period of my life. You have never even seen it, and yet you are disappointed because I decline to give it up in your favour. And you must remember that you ladies, after all, are total strangers to me."

"But we're not asking for charity, Mr. Judge. We would take the place at your figure, even if it were a trifle unreasonable. If you don't mean to live there again yourself—and you seem very doubtful about it—surely there can't be any object in refusing to allow other people to occupy it? if you don't want to sell it outright, you might consent to let it for a term of years?"

Judge smiled uneasily. "It's very painful to me to have to go on refusing. I must admit I don't quite understand your eagerness in the matter. Not having seen Runhill Court, you don't even know that it will suit your requirements."

"We have seen it. Mr. Stokes took us over. It will suit our requirements perfectly."

"Oh. . . I had no idea. Mr. Stokes said nothing to me in his letter about that. However, there's no harm done."

"My aunt and I are quite harmless persons."

"I regard it as an honour to the house. May I ask whether you saw the whole of it?"

She imperceptibly drew a little nearer, so that the perfume of her clothes began to insinuate itself into his consciousness.

"Except prohibited parts."

"It's a pity I wasn't told beforehand, Miss Loment. I could have shown you over personally."

Their eyes chanced to meet. Isbel smiled, and looked down at her lap, while Judge coloured faintly.

"That would have been nice."

"At all events, you would have had the advantage of seeing the so-called 'prohibited parts' as well. I might still hold that out as an inducement for a second visit, but I suspect you would think it not worth while?"

She began biting her chain. After a pause, she said: "Something might be arranged, perhaps. I should love to see it again. My best friend's coming down for the week-end, and I could bring her with me—if you feel you could endure the society of a couple of frivolous girls for half-a-day. You'd be quite safe, Mr. Judge; Blanche is married, and I am to be soon."

"Your aunt would come, too?"

"I haven't the slightest objection, if you can persuade her."

"I have first to meet her."

"Then dine with us here one night. Let me think. . . Friday would do, if you can manage it?" She gave him a friendly look. "We can discuss the programme at table. Blanche's husband is Mr. Stokes' brother; they're both coming down." . . . Hesitating, and blushing a little—"Of course, *their* company wouldn't be inflicted on you at Runhill."

Judge also hesitated. "It's most kind of you; but how do I know that your aunt may not have objections to sitting down to table with a stranger, who is not even obliging?"

"The invitation is mine, Mr. Judge."

"Then, of course, I shouldn't know how to refuse, even if I wanted to. A charming invitation demands a graceful acceptance. I shall be delighted to come."

"At seven. . . But will you have to come all the way from town?"

"No—my headquarters are at Worthing for the time being. I have to be near Runhill to look after things. I can quite easily run over."

"Then it's a fixed engagement. . . And meanwhile, you still remain adamant?"

Her own question seemed to agitate her, for her bosom rose and fell. Judge summed her up in his mind as a spoilt and capricious young woman of fortune, who was totally unaccustomed to being baulked even in her most unnecessary whims.

"It's exceedingly unpleasant for me, Miss Loment, but I'm afraid I must reply in the affirmative. If circumstances permit me later on to change my decision. . ."

"It would be too late. In point of fact, the moment my aunt has your verdict we shall leave Brighton. We're only waiting for that. But I shall leave you to tell her yourself, so as not to interfere with our little pleasure-party."

"Then your permanent residence is not in Brighton?"

"Oh, no."

Judge contracted his brows. "It's a strange fact, but it has always been my disappointing lot to fall in with really pleasant acquaintances just when it is too late."

"It does seem to happen like that very often. Perhaps it's because the pleasure doesn't have time to wear off. . . Of course, if you were to leave the question of your house in abeyance we might still see something of each other—especially since you are staying so close at hand. But that wouldn't be quite the right thing, I expect?"

"Mrs. Moor would hardly consent to postpone it indefinitely."

"Then that's no good. . . Anyhow, don't write her, Mr. Judge. She can very well wait till Friday."

He got up to go. Isbel rose, too, and held out her hand. It was white and elegant in shape, but was ink-stained from her correspondence. Judge continued holding it while he went on talking.

"I've no right to ask such a thing, Miss Loment, but I'm interested, and perhaps you won't mind telling me. You said you are to be married; is it, by any chance, to my friend Mr. Stokes?"

"Yes." She coloured nervously, and withdrew her hand.

"Thanks! And my I venture to add my congratulations to those you have doubtless received from friends of longer standing? He is a very pleasant, sensible young fellow, and, from what I know of him, will certainly make an admirable husband."

"Thank you, Mr. Judge! My only fear is that I may not make as admirable a wife."

Judge laughed courteously. "All I have to say to that is that I consider Mr. Stokes a very lucky individual—very lucky indeed!"

Isbel felt so strangely confused that she could not bring out another word. They passed into the hall, where Judge, with leisurely dignity, put on his gloves and buttoned his coat, while the girl watched him. At last he bade her a smiling "Good-day," and went out stiffly through the swing-doors into the rain. She remained for a moment standing by the office, looking after him with a peculiar little smile.

On arriving upstairs, her aunt gave her a keen stare.

"You've got a very flushed very, child."

"I ran upstairs."

"What a long time you've been with that man. What did he want?"

"Oh, he's frantically long-winded. The long and short of it is, I've asked him to dinner on Friday, to meet you. It seems he'd rather discuss it with you personally."

"Upon my soul! Why in the world should we dine him? . . . I had a presentiment you would do something silly."

"Oh, he's perfectly presentable. Besides, he'll be glad to meet Marshall again. I had to make some definite arrangement."

Mrs. Moor growled in her throat. "Well, the point is, are we to get the house, or not?"

"I fancy he still hasn't made up his mind," replied Isbel indifferently.

Her aunt made sundry inarticulate sounds, indicative of her vexation, and prepared to rise.

VII

The Dinner-Party

At seven o'clock on Friday evening the party of six sat down to table in the public room. Judge found himself between the two girls, while Mrs. Moor had the two brothers for neighbors; Isbel faced Marshall across the table, and Blanche her own husband.

Blanche, the tall, pale, slender, fashionable blonde, looked a creature of fine clay in her dinner-frock of foam-blue and silver. She drew many glances from the other diners in the room, and for a long time Marshall and Judge entered into a sort of competition for her favour. Isbel was amused, rather than otherwise. With regard to "personal property," there was a perfect understanding between her friend and herself, and she had already, earlier in the day, intimated to Blanche what her wishes were concerning Judge.

While waiting for her to disentangle herself, she occupied the time by chatting with Roger on indifferent topics. There could be nothing very exciting in that; he was a nice man, but she was quite well aware that for him only one woman in the world existed—namely, his own wife. His profession was historical research—fortunately, he did not rely upon it for an income—but, as everyone possesses a dual nature, his favourite role in society was that of Mephistopheles, which he undertook consistently. He was four years older than Marshall, and not unlike him in person, though built on a small scale. He had the same broad, pugnacious, good-humoured face, but it was more humorous and sympathetic, and the eyes were livelier.

Isbel's new wine-red gown had the effect of investing her face with a strange luminous pallor, which almost took the place of beauty. At intervals Judge turned to her in a puzzled way, but Blanche's fascinations were more obvious, and the pear was not yet ripe.

It was not until the meal was halfway through and a few bottles had been emptied, that the talk became loud and general. Mrs. Moor was fidgeting about Runhill Court, and began to think that she would never have an opportunity of opening that business. She could hardly start negotiations at table, but she told herself that at least she ought to try to find out how things lay. At the first lull in the conversation, therefore, she addressed Judge directly by name, and when he looked up, rather surprised, she introduced the subject of Sherrup.

Judge raised his brows. "I know who you mean, but we've never met. There has been some correspondence between us. He was making the trip to England, and wished to visit my place. It seems his wife's people at one time owned the estate."

"So he told us. It was actually in your house that we met him."

"Thumping your piano, incidentally," added Marshall.

Judge shot him a glance of inquiry.

"Hammering out Mendelssohn," explained the underwriter.

"It was one of Beethoven's Symphonies, to be exact," corrected Isbel, with a smile. "The Seventh. Are you musical, Mr. Judge?"

"Not very, I fear. You, of course, are?"

"But why 'of course'? Am I so transparent a person?"

Roger tossed off a full glass of Sauterne. "Some women *have* accomplishments. Billy is one of the latter sort."

"Honey with a sting in it, Roger. Those of us who have no brains you are kind enough to console with fascination. But perhaps I have neither."

"Or perhaps both," suggested Judge, gallantly. "I for one, see no reason why they should not go together. Many of the cleverest women in history have been the most fascinating."

"But history has been written by men, and men aren't the most enlightened critics where women are concerned. All that will have to be re-written by qualified feminine experts some day."

Judge laughed. "But, in point of fact, men happen to be the best critics of feminine human nature. A woman's natural impulse is to look for faults in her sisters; a man's first thought is to look for noble qualities."

"It may be very chivalrous, but I don't call it criticism," rejoined Isbel quickly. "You're not in the least likely ever to understand a woman's character that way."

"If faults constitute a character—no. But my contention is that it's this constant dwelling on faults which obscures our view of a woman's real underlying nature. In this sense men are the best observers of your sex."

"Let me translate," put in Roger. "It's good policy to credit a woman with virtues, for if she hasn't got them already, she will have as soon as she clearly understands that other people believe that she has. Does that go?"

His wife answered: "If you praise a woman's frock, she will probably like to go on wearing it. Why should it be different with a virtue? Because you haven't worn a thing for a long while, it doesn't follow, when you do wear it, that it isn't your own rightful property."

"Then there are no counterfeit qualities?" demanded Isbel.

"None which cannot be easily detected," said Judge. "To extend Mrs. Stokes' comparison: a borrowed or stolen garment can in most cases be discovered to be so by the misfit. In life, it isn't difficult to distinguish between true and false."

"Does that apply to everything—every quality?"

"Undoubtedly, in my opinion."

"To the relation between men and women?"

"Certainly. Genuine love—for I take it you mean that—would be the most difficult thing in the world to simulate."

"*Really?*"

"Almost an impossibility, if only men and women were not so anxious to be deceived."

"Yet coquettes have existed, and still exist."

Judge lifted his glass with a hand steady as a rock, and examined its contents against the light meditatively.

"Don't misunderstand me, Miss Loment. I don't assert that an infatuated man couldn't be hoodwinked by a clever woman, if she made it her business. All I say is, if he is dubious about her good faith, tests exist."

"What tests?"

"A coquette, for instance, would know how to flatter his vanity and use her eyes to the best effect, but it's extremely unlikely that she would consent to throw overboard all other society for his. That would be one test. . . And then there's the question of sacrifice. Is she, not only ready, but eager, to sacrifice her own happiness for his, not in one way or on one occasion, but in all their relations and at all times? . . ."

"Most excellent tests!" said Roger, with twinkling eyes. "If fulfilled satisfactorily, the fair lady in question might be safely set down as mortally wounded, and our friend could go full steam ahead with every assurance of eventually leading her to the altar."

Blanche leant her beautiful arm on the table and propped her face with her fingers.

"But do you insist, Mr. Judge, that every romance is imperfect which doesn't exhibit these extreme symptoms on both sides?"

"As a matter of fact, I wasn't thinking of romance, in the common acceptance of the term, Mrs. Stokes. There are deep, and possibly painful, transactions of the heart to which the term 'romance' would be quite inadequate."

There was a general silence, while the waiter removed the course. The subject was not resumed across the table, but Isbel followed it up with Judge, in a low voice.

"You seem to speak from experience, Mr. Judge?"

"A man of my age must possess a large accumulation of experience, Miss Loment, but it needn't necessarily be personal experience."

"In that case you are to be congratulated, for it can't be a happy condition—this deep passion you have just described."

He toyed with the stem of his empty glass. "Only certain natures have a capacity for it, perhaps, and they perhaps have an inward tormenting craving for it. It's very difficult to lay down a law as to what is good, and what is not good."

"And I think women must have it more than men."

He glanced at her swiftly. "As the self-sacrificing sex, you mean?"

"No, I don't mean that. I mean, as the sex which worships the heart, and believes it higher than the highest morality."

"That's true."

"And the worst of it is," went on Isbel, speaking still lower, "no woman can feel really safe until she has experienced this feeling you speak of." She uttered a nervous laugh. "Someone else may turn up, who will prove to her how mistakenly she has been living. . . But, of course, I know nothing about it. Girls get all sorts of queer fancies in their heads, and that's because they don't live in the real world."

"The wisest course is not to think about such things. By a useful provision of nature, passion comes to comparatively few, and there's no reason for anyone to suppose that he or she is one of the tragic band. The chances are infinitely against it."

"Yes, of course—that's the only sensible way to think. . . I hope you're not offended by my breach of decorum in discussing such matters?"

"How could I be?"

"Then don't let's say anymore. My aunt's watching us. . . Apropos, have you spoken to her about Runhill yet?"

"I've had no real opportunity up to the present."

"Is it really necessary to this evening?"

"Possibly not, if it could be avoided."

"Will you leave it to me?"

"Willingly; but if she questions me, I must answer her."

"Of course, but don't be precipitate." A quick smile. "I don't want to return to town yet."

"You find Brighton attractive?"

"It has attractions."

Judge's cream-ice stood in front of him untouched.

"The place itself, or the connections you have formed here?"

"The place itself is horrid."

Meanwhile Blanche had been exchanging words with Marshall.

"I want to get Mr. Judge to show us over his house—myself and Roger, I mean. What's the best way to go to work?"

She did not explain that the idea was Isbel's, and she herself only the friendly medium.

"Ask him, of course," said Marshall. "He's quite an obliging old sort."

"You go back on Monday, don't you?"

"Yes. Why?"

"I thought we might fix Monday. You wouldn't want to see the place again, would you?"

"I want Billy to come with us, though. I expect you wouldn't take it in bad part for once—running off like that without you, I mean?"

"Lord, no!—why should I? Very glad if you can make a decent day of it. I'd take lunch and make it a picnic, if I were you."

"Good man! . . . Then here goes for the lord of the manor! . . ."

Judge, having concluded his talk with Isbel, had mechanically turned to his other neighbour. Blanche met his eye with a soft, disarming smile.

"I'm glad you've remembered me, Mr. Judge. I'm in a difficulty."

"That's woeful news."

"My husband and I are madly jealous. We're the only ones here who haven't seen your much-talked-about house. I daren't proffer a direct request, for fear of being snubbed."

"You pay me a very bad compliment, Mrs. Stokes; I didn't' know I possessed such a forbidding exterior."

"Then, may we come for one day?"

"I shall regard it as a distinguished honour. Pray fix your own day."

"We go back on Tuesday. Monday perhaps. . . ?"

"On Monday it shall be. I'll bring my car over for you. At what hour?"

"But really, we wouldn't dream of putting you to all that trouble."

"It will be a very great pleasure. Unhappily, it's only a four-seater, so I fear the party would have to be separated."

"Mr. Stokes—Mr. *Marshall* Stokes"—she laughed—"can't come, for the simple reason that he's due back to work on Monday. What about you, Mrs. Moor?"

"I've seen the house already, my dear. Isbel will to with you, no doubt."

"Will you, Billy?"

Isbel appeared to hesitate. . . "I don't know that I care to, thanks. I've seen it, too, you know."

"Oh, I'd go, Isbel," urged Marshall. "The summer's practically through, and you won't get many more decent spins. I'd squeeze in, myself, if I hadn't to go back."

"Mr. Judge may object to so many women."

"Surely you weren't waiting for my formal invitation, Miss Loment? I shall feel extremely hurt if you refuse."

"Very well—I'll come," said Isbel quietly, bending her head over her plate, with a very slight access of colour. Judge marvelled at her seeming reluctance to her own scheme, but he somehow felt pleased. It was flattering to be behind the scenes with her.

"Then that's all right," said Blanche. "What time will you come and collect us, Mr. Judge?"

"You shall decide. I reserve the whole of Monday."

Isbel leant over in front of Judge to address her friend. "You don't realise, dear, that he's staying at Worthing—ten miles away. We're all being deplorably inconsiderate."

"Five miles per beauteous lady is not an extravagant addition to the petrol allowance." Roger had not spared the bottle. "How say you, Judge?"

"As you say, sir, it's not worth considering—especially when I have the pleasure of your society thrown in."

Blanche's brow was puckered, as though an idea had occurred to her. "I wonder, Mr. Judge, if it would be possible to arrange a picnic-luncheon on the grounds—or the house itself, according to the weather? It would be rather jolly. The hotel people here would make us up a hamper."

"Not at all," said Judge. "I'll see to that myself. It's a capital suggestion, for it will give us more time to look round."

"But really, that's the woman's department, and we can't allow you."

"I insist, Mrs. Stokes. I'm an obstinate man, and there's no more to be said. I'll bring the hamper along with me, and call for you at. . . ten—eleven. . . ?"

"Call it eleven," said Roger. "I'm a late riser. We'll lunch first, and saunter through the house afterwards. Don't forget the wine."

The girls scolded him; he defended himself with new jokes and drank off another glass. The coffee came on. The younger people lit cigarettes, but Judge reserved his after-dinner cigar till later.

Mrs. Moor, who had been silent throughout the meal, grew more irritated as she saw the minutes fly by without bringing her any nearer to an exchange of views with Judge. She momentarily expected to see him rise from the table and take his departure, leaving her still in ignorance of his intentions. Perhaps it wasn't deliberate avoidance of the topic on his part, but it began to look very much like it. Isbel glanced at her aunt anxiously; she read her thoughts with perfect distinctness.

"You're very quiet tonight, aunt."

"You others are doing quite well without my help."

"Mr. Judge has asked me to intercede for him."

Mrs. Moor stiffened. "What is it?"

"He wants another extension of time, before giving you a final decision."

"Really, Mr. Judge. . ."

"It can't be helped, aunt, and we mustn't be stupid about it. How long do you want, Mr. Judge?"

"Shall we say a fortnight?" His manner was strangely embarrassed. "I may not need all of that. If not, I would notify you at once."

Mrs. Moor eyed him sternly. "A fortnight, then. You quite understand my inquiries for a house are continuing in the meantime?"

"That is but fair."

"A firm offer on my part wouldn't expedite matters, I presume?"

"I regret to say 'no.' The financial question does not arise at present."

Baffled by his formal tone and the distant gravity of his demeanour, she retired into silence, to nurse her displeasure. Isbel turned in her seat to glance at Judge, and uttered a quiet little laugh.

"I'm afraid you won't be altogether in her good graces now. It's my fault."

"Since I have the misfortune to be obliged to displease one of you, I would rather it were she."

"I know that." Her voice was very low, but he caught the words, and his face took on a deeper colour.

"How do you know it?"

"Because we are already friends."

Both turned away, moved by the same impulse. A minute later, however, Isbel whispered to him again:

"In case I ever need it, what is your address at Worthing?"

"The Metropole."

She thanked him, and turned finally to Roger.

"Isbel seems to find a lot to talk about with Judge," Marshall had just been remarking to his sister-in-law.

"No cause for alarm, dear boy—she only wants his house."

"Do you tell me she's deliberately laying herself out to be pleasant. . . ?"

"Don't you ever use diplomacy in *your* trade? One has to fight with what weapons one's got. You're in on this too, Marshall. I suppose you do want to get Billy to yourself one day, don't you? Well, then—hurry up and find Mrs. Moor a house."

Shortly afterward the party rose from table, and Judge immediately took his departure.

VIII

THE PICNIC

At mid-day on Monday, Judge's Daimler pulled up outside the hall porch at Runhill Court. Roger jumped out and assisted the girls to alight, after which Judge himself got down. Beneath the motoring wraps, Blanche and Isbel wore light summer dresses, for, although it was already October, the sky was cloudless and the sun hot. All congratulated themselves on the happy selection of such a day for their excursion.

"Where do we go?" laughed Blanche.

Judge was struggling to get out the baskets. He deposited the second one on the ground and dusted his hands.

"We're going to picnic in a very charming spot, Mrs. Stokes. Leave it to me. Mr. Stokes, as the younger man, the bigger basket falls to you."

"Thanks! How far is it?"

"Come on!" said his wife. "Never mind how far—we'll all give a hand. You and I will tackle the big one, Roger; Mr. Judge can take the smaller; Billy can carry the rug."

"Won't you leave your wraps, though?" inquired Judge. "It seems to me that once or twice I've half caught a glimpse of something very enticing underneath. The grass should be moderately dry."

"You haven't forgotten the wine, Judge?" demanded Roger. "If I work, I want pay. The girls' frocks leave me uninspired, more especially as my wife's hasn't been settled for yet. I don't stir a step till I know what's in that basket."

"This is a picnic, not an orgy," said Blanche reprovingly.

Judge lifted the smaller hamper. "I saw the wine go in, and I believe it's very good stuff."

"But you're a horrid sybarite, Roger," put in Isbel. "Why is it that strong and healthy young men are invariably the most self-indulgent?" She removed her wrap and flung it carelessly in the car; Blanche followed suit.

"I like that. You women pass your whole lives delighting your souls with fine raiment, and then you have the cool impudence to rebuke us for indulgence."

"Personally, I regard feminine adornment not only as justifiable, but as a public duty," remarked Judge. "One can hardly say as much for the private pleasures of men."

Roger chuckled. "If you carry on in that strain you'll make yourself popular. Look at the girls, drinking it all in with open mouths."

"Mr. Judge is a knight," said Isbel coldly. "You are only a jester, Roger."

"But is it good to be a knight, fair lady?"

"So it seems to my poor intelligence."

"'Tis a most dangerous profession. Your knight is a flatterer. But your flatterer may well end by becoming regarded as personal property. I shall remain a jester, I think."

They started off, by Judge's direction, along the terrace which skirted the front of the house. Blanche and Roger went on ahead, bearing the larger hamper between them, while Isbel and Judge fell behind, the latter carrying the small basket.

Isbel looked pensive. After a minute she said: "That last remark of Roger's was as bitter as it was untrue. It makes out that we women are incapable of discriminating between personal and impersonal flattery. It isn't words that we go by; it's the man himself—his character."

"I imagine so. But, still, pleasant words lead to friendship."

"Sometimes, perhaps. The best kind of friendship's more than empty compliments."

"And what do you understand by the best kind of friendship—between persons of opposite sex?"

She coloured faintly. "It is one of those things which are more easily known to oneself than defined."

"For a friendship like that requires great tact, and tact is not of the brain. It is very delicate instinct."

"Yes. And that's why I am so glad to have *you* for a friend Mr. Judge—for I feel certain that you possess this. . . *tact*, in the highest degree. . . However, it would make no difference. We shall soon see no more of each other."

"Can't we arrange to the contrary?"

"How? We shall be leaving this part of the country almost directly, and you know we don't know the same people. It's extremely unlikely we shall ever meet again."

"In plain language, Miss Loment—pardon me, I must speak openly—my house is the price of the continuance of your friendship? That is what you mean?"

"The statement is yours, not mine. I don't presume to flatter myself that my humble acquaintance is worth more to you than your house. I should indeed be an egotist."

"You mustn't say that, Miss Loment. My interests are very complicated; it isn't at all so simple as that. Please say no more at present. . . Of one thing you can be quite assured—I certainly do *not* wish to lose your friendship, and if it can in anyway be arranged. . ."

"Oh, it doesn't matter," said Isbel. . . "Let me relieve you with that basket."

They had reached the east end of the house. Blanche and Roger were standing waiting at the angle, ignorant which way to proceed; they had set down the hamper.

"Which way now?" demanded Blanche.

"We'll change over," said Isbel. "The men can take the big basket and we'll bring up the rear. I'll have the other basket, Blanche, and you can carry the rug."

Roger, with a groan, prepared to stoop again. "Don't say it's far!"

"About two hundred yards," replied Judge. "The spot I have in mind is at the bottom of that field you see there."

Isbel was staring up at the house; she pointed a finger towards a gable. "Isn't that the window of the East Room, Mr. Judge?"

"It is; but what makes you ask?"

As she was about to reply, Blanche suddenly broke in:

"I didn't know the house had four storeys. You said only three, Billy."

"There are only three."

"Four, darling!"

"No three. Count again." The men confirmed her statement. Blanche did count again, and now made it only three. She confessed her blunder, laughed and promptly allowed the incident to pass from her mind. Isbel stole a glance at Judge, who was thoughtfully stroking his chin, while gazing at the house.

Nothing more was said till they commenced the descent of the steeply sloping lawn, the lower end of which adjoined the field. Judge and Roger went ahead.

"Did you really think you saw four storeys?" asked Isbel with assumed carelessness.

"Yes, I did. Why?"

"Oh, nothing."

"What makes you so keen on that house, Billy? I know it isn't only on your aunt's account."

Isbel laughed. "You're developing into a very suspicious person. What other motive could I possibly have? Considering the short time I should have to live there, it isn't worth my while to get excited on my own account. It's a quaint old place, I admit."

"Have you got round Mr. Judge yet?"

"Not yet."

"Don't make poor old Marshall too jealous, that's all."

"Really, you say the most weird things. What do you imagine I'm doing? You might give me credit for a small modicum of self-respect."

"All right, but men are strange animals. The flash-point is very low in some of them. Don't forget that."

They reached the bottom of the lawn, and then had to cross a low stile into the field. The descent continued, but not so sharply. The field lay fallow; a fringe of elms bounded it on three sides, while on the fourth was a wood, towards which they made their way. The sun blazed, and the flies were troublesome. Roger looked back, to point out to the girls some swallows which had not yet departed.

"Why should you think he's that sort of man?" demanded Isbel.

"Oh, my dear, I've caught him looking rather strangely at you once or twice. Men are men and you can't make anything else of them. He knows you're engaged, of course?"

"My dear Blanche! . . ."

"Well, I won't say anything more. You know best. Only, do be very, very careful."

Isbel maintained an indignant silence until they neared the lower end of the field. The men, who had increased their distance, kept glancing over their shoulders by way of protest against the girls' leisurely pace.

"Surely, I'm not asking very much of him, Blanche? If he doesn't want to live in the house himself, he might just as well let us have it. Aunt will pay him his full price."

"No doubt he's an excellent business man," said Blanche enigmatically.

They rejoined the others at the spot selected for lunch.

The rug was spread on the grass, and the hampers were unpacked. While Roger busied himself with carving the pheasants and uncorking the hock, the girls neatly set out rolls, pastries, fruit, etc., and Judge made himself generally useful. They lunched in full sunlight in the field, by the side of a rather romantic little stream. This brook separated them from the steeply-ascending wood beyond, and—only an inch or so in depth—was so beautifully transparent, and flowed over its clean bed of pebbles with so musical a gurgle, that Isbel's spirits imperceptibly became tranquillised. They were in the trough of the two hillsides, and the house was out of sight.

"This licks friend Omar, I fancy," said Roger, vigorously attacking his half-bird. "For one flask of rotten syrup we have three bottles of the genuine stuff, for a loaf of bread we have game, and for 'thou' we have two. Can't you compose a verse for the occasion, Judge?"

"I strongly protest against figuring in as a 'thou,'" said Isbel, coolly. "Those times are past forever. Henceforward men are going to exist for us, not we for them."

"Capital! You have my fullest consent. I haven't the faintest shadow of an objection to assisting to change a pretty woman's wilderness into a paradise. Choose forthright between Judge and me."

"This is the grave historian, Mr. Judge, who spends his days in the dusty old reading-room at the British Museum."

"All the more justification for letting it go now, my dear," returned Roger. "After long enforced spells of hobnobbing with kings, heroes, and politicians, nature cries out for a little human intercourse with simple Jane and pleasant Muriel."

"Which of us is simple Jane?" demanded Isbel coldly.

"Simple Jane is the one with the fewer ideas, and pleasant Muriel is the one with the greater number of smiles. You can fight it out between you. . . Now leave me alone. I'm going to be busy."

"Mr. Judge, are you going to let this unparalleled rudeness pass without rebuke?"

Judge threw out his hands. "What can I do, dear lady? He leaves nothing to catch hold of. Personally, I think it is a very cunning device on his part to draw more smiles from both of you."

"Are you asserting that we are being dull?" asked Blanche, retaining her fork with its fragment of food in mid-air, as she stared at him with wide eyes.

"Not dull, certainly. Perhaps a shade more thoughtful than the occasion warrants. I was wondering whether possibly I had said or done something to offend you?"

"How absurd!" exclaimed Isbel. "*You* of all people."

"Guilty conscience, Billy," said Roger, with his mouth full. "He's done something, but isn't sure if it's been spotted. Out with it, Judge!"

"No, no, that doesn't arise. Since Miss Loment assures me to the contrary, it would be ungallant to carry the matter further."

"Coward! . . . *Moi*, I offend Billy on an average once a fortnight throughout the year. A capital creature, but slightly hasty-tempered."

"You've never once upset me in your life, my good man. Whenever you get beyond a certain level of offensiveness, I can see only the funny side. . . Besides, that's not the point. We were discussing Mr. Judge, not you. To be offended is to be disappointed, and what right have I to be disappointed at anything Mr. Judge may say or do, seeing that I am practically unacquainted with his character?"

Blanche looked up sharply. Judge's face took on a deep flush.

"As far as that goes," he said, after a moment's pause, "I don't know that I'm very different from what I seem."

"That must mean, you never do unexpected things? Everything proceeds with you according to your physiognomy? You must be a very happy man, Mr. Judge."

"And why should he do unexpected things?" asked Roger. "The unexpected is sometimes charming, but nearly always idiotic. Give me a man who can explain his actions afterwards."

"Yes, I suppose that's the man's ideal. It isn't the woman's. We like men who obey the heart occasionally, instead of the head. It's stupid, of course, and we can't defend it, but somehow that's the kind of men we should prefer to have for a friend."

"And why?"

"Because we women count generosity as a virtue, Roger."

Roger drank, and wiped his mouth.

"Then, is an irresponsible person necessarily generous?"

"No, but all I mean is, we admire people who place friendship first, self-interest second."

"It appears that the fair Billy doth know a thing or two!"

Isbel wriggled her shoulders impatiently. "I don't want gifts from friends, but I do want friends who aren't afraid of giving. Surely that distinction is obvious?"

"Quite. What you are suffering from is acute *romance*. Such interesting persons no longer walk this hard, cold world of ours, if they have ever done so. A man's best friend is his bank balance. You may take that as an axiom."

"I fully believe it." Isbel raised her glass to the level of her face. "So here's long life to money, property, and self!"

DAVID LINDSAY

"And wine, and women, and smiles, and the blessed sunshine—everything, in short, that makes life worth living! And *a bas* all metaphysical discussions between living men and women! A special staff of professors has been retained by the world to deal with all that trash."

Having emptied his glass at a gulp, Roger pulled out a cigar, which he proceeded to cut and light with relish. Judge regarded him smilingly.

"You never take things seriously, Mr. Stokes?"

"Yes, my work. But after work I believe in play."

"And no doubt you deserve it. Does he deserve it, Mrs. Stokes?"

"He works like a nigger, I fancy," answered Blanche, negligently. "It runs in the family. His brother Marshall's rapidly acquiring a fortune, and Roger is rapidly acquiring a reputation. Sometimes I feel I should like it to be the other way round."

"So Mr. Marshall Stokes is really clever?"

"They tell me he's a sort of little Napoleon, in his way. Billy's a lucky girl, whether she knows it or not."

"And Mr. Stokes is lucky, too."

"No, no—no gamble about it at all. A man is not a man till he gets married, and if he's unhappy afterwards, it's in all cases entirely his own fault. Look at Mr. Roger Stokes here. He's thoroughly contented with life—it's true he's been a trifle spoilt. . . Mr. Stokes, your health! . . . You must come to all my future picnics, if I am fortunate enough to have anymore—if only for the sake of your high spirits."

"Then, on the whole, I've given greater satisfaction than the girls?"

"That I didn't say. Somethings are outside praise, as you know— the glorious sun, for example. You're the wine of the party, Mr. Stokes, while the ladies are the sunshine."

As the afternoon wore on, Isbel developed a headache. She withdrew from the talk, and kept glancing at her wrist-watch; it was nearing two o'clock.

"You look pale, Billy," said Blanche at last.

"My head aches a little."

Everyone manifested sympathy. They decided to pack up and go, and meanwhile Isbel was made to sit in the shade of the trees. When finally they were ready to start for the house, she found herself with empty hands, walking beside Judge.

"May I speak, or would you rather be quiet?" he asked, after a few paces.

"No; please do."

"It's about my house. Why do you want it so badly, Miss Loment?"

She was silent for quite a long time.

"Perhaps it's your friendship I want, and not your house."

"Ah! . . . But since when. . ."

"I don't know. These feelings grow, don't they?"

"Yes. . . but why my friendship? . . . How have I deserved this? . . ."

"Then perhaps it *is* your house I want, after all. . . Really, Mr. Judge, I know as little about this as you." She lowered her tone. "Of course, you know you are an exceptional man? You can understand it must be very flattering for a girl to be friends with such a man."

His face grew dark, but he said nothing till they were nearing the stile, where the others stood waiting for them. Then:

"You have my permission to tell your aunt that she may have Runhill Court at an agreed figure. I won't stand out any longer."

"And this offer is. . . unconditional?"

"Yes, unconditional."

"You clearly understand—oh, I can't say it. . ."

"You need not try. I clearly understand everything, and the offer is entirely without conditions."

"Then I will accept it," said Isbel, in a nearly inaudible voice.

IX

What Happened in the Second Room

As they trooped into the ancient, strangely-coloured hall their voices instinctively became lower and joking ceased. Blanche drew her friend aside.

"It's a lovely place, Billy! . . . Well, did you speak to him again?"

"Yes, it's all right—he's going to let us have it."

"How did you manage it?"

"I didn't manage it at all; the offer came from him."

"Really?"

"Certainly—why shouldn't it? So now we shall live here, I suppose."

"Congratulations, my dear! . . . I expect you'll have to see quite a lot of him after this? You took that into consideration, of course?"

"Why do you dislike him so much?"

"I neither like nor dislike him. I'm only afraid you may have to pay a rather high price for your house, that's all. However, it's *your* funeral. . ."

Blanche forthwith turned to Judge, to express her astonishment at the beauty of the hall. It looked even weirder than usual, by reason of the circumstance that the sun's rays now penetrated the windows obliquely, so that one half of the place was in shadow. Judge responded to her with somewhat worried courtesy. Meanwhile Isbel seated herself in a wicker chair, with her back to the fireplace.

"Is the headache worse?" asked Roger, quietly and kindly.

"It isn't any better, Roger." As the others came up: "I wonder if you would all mind seeing the house without me? I hate being a wet blanket."

"What do you propose doing, then?" asked Blanche.

"I'll stop here; my head's going like an engine. I've seen everything before."

"Except that one room," Judge reminded her. "Still, there's absolutely nothing to see there."

"What room is that?" asked Blanche.

"A room on the top floor," explained Isbel. "Supposed to be haunted—isn't it, Mr. Judge?"

"I don't know where that information comes from, I'm sure. Foolish tales may be told of it, as of any other room."

Blanche laughed. "A real live ghost, Mr. Judge?"

"I hope it's a classic example, but I really know nothing about it."

"How thrilling? You'll take *us* there?"

"Certainly, if you wish it."

But, first of all, they decided to complete their inspection of the apartments on the ground floor. Isbel remained sitting while the others wandered about the hall. The almost incessant drone of Judge's voice, as he explained his property, detail by detail, began to exercise a soporific effect upon her, and she had a hard task to keep her eyes open. . .

She must have dozed, for she awoke to consciousness with a start. She was alone in the hall. Her friends were still somewhere on the lower floor; she could hear their voices sounding from one of the rooms in the back of the house. The words were indistinguishable, but Judge's rumbling tones were nearly continuous, while Blanche's high-pitched organ supplied an occasional punctuation. She thought how singular it was that a woman's voice should always sound so absurdly shrill when heard from another room in conjunction with a man's.

She sat up sharply and rearranged her skirt. Without her being aware of the fact, her foot was tapping the floor rapidly in nervous agitation. Before going upstairs they would have to return to the hall. They might reappear at any moment, and until they were safely away in the upper part of the house she dared not risk turning in her chair—to see what was behind her. . . If *those stairs* should already be there!

When, shortly afterwards, the door of the dining-room was thrown open and her friends re-entered the hall in a cluster, bringing with them a clatter of conversation, Isbel smiled towards them, but made no offer to rise.

"Aha! She's awake," exclaimed Roger.

"Did you expect to find me asleep, then?"

"You were slumbering beatifically when we left you. We went out on tiptoes, like a trio of conspirators. Endorse me, Judge."

"Well, what do you think of it all, Blanche, as far as you've seen?"

"It's a perfectly wonderful house. So picturesque and quiet, and so full of shadows. Won't you come over the rest with us now?"

"No, thanks. I'd better keep still, I think."

Judge pulled out a gold half-hunter. "What shan't be a great while. It's a quarter to three. It ought not to take us above an hour, I fancy. You don't mind waiting that time?"

"No, no—only do go!"

Before departing, Roger lit a cigarette.

"Have one, to pass the time away, Billy?"

"Perhaps I will."

The first match went out, and she reached her hand for the box.

"I've seen steadier hands than yours," remarked Roger.

She passed back the box without a word, retained the lighted cigarette in her mouth, and suffered her hand to remain motionless on her lap. Blanche and Judge were already at the foot of the staircase, and Roger hastened after them. Isbel gave a noiseless sigh, smoking on nervously.

From her seat she could hear her friends debating on the upper landing where they should go first. Judge suggested the first-floor apartments, but Blanche insisted on the haunted room. Apparently she gained her way, for a minute later their footsteps sounded on the upper staircase, leading to the top of the house. Their voices sank to a confused murmur, which grew lower and lower, until at last absolute silence reigned.

At the end of three minutes or so, Isbel rose suddenly, overturning the chair in her vehemence. Her eyes swiftly fastened themselves on the wall next to the fireplace. . . And then she gave a silent laugh of reaction, for she at once realised how unnecessary her impatience had been. Not only was that staircase there, directly confronting her, but how could it *help* being there?—it was so manifestly solid and tangible, it was so essential a part of the structure of the hall. . . Truly, it was most puzzling that she had not noticed it on their entrance a short time ago, and that none of the party had called attention to it, but it was out of the question to go against the evidence of her senses. The staircase was made of wood, it had been constructed by human hands, and it ascended to a different part of the same house. There was nothing mystical or unnatural about it; it was a straight-forward piece of work, intended for everyday use. And in fact, she had used it. If she hadn't perfectly well remembered that, she would certainly not have plotted and planned to be there that afternoon.

More minutes passed before she could bring herself to move. Covering her eyes with her hand, she made a violent effort to recall what had taken place before; it was both odd and exasperating that it should have so completely escaped her. She distinctly recollected her impressions while standing with her foot on the first step, but after that all was oblivion, until she had been in the act of redescending into the hall. What could possibly be the cause of this most unpleasant failure of memory? . . . Perhaps the atmosphere of that upper part of the building was hypnotic? That, however, would only be explaining one mystery by another, for what kind of rooms could they be which had the effect of drugging the brain to permanent forgetfulness? But perhaps she had dreamt it all, and was still dreaming? Or she might be suffering from hallucination, suggested by Judge's story? . . . She had never felt more sane, wide awake, or rational in her life. The explanation could not be that. . .

Time was creeping on. She looked upwards towards the gallery, and listened intently, with held breath. There was not a sound; the others evidently were still on the top floor. She stepped noiselessly across to the bottom of the staircase, and began to ascend. Again the thrill of adventure seized her which she had experienced on the former occasion. She felt that she was visiting an unknown region of the house, where strange discoveries awaited her. . .

Almost immediately she started to remember. She could not recall everything at once, but had to piece it together, as one pieces together an old and buried event in one's career. At the head of these stairs there should be an ante-room, with three doors. Through one of these doors she had passed. In the room beyond she had seen. . . a wall-mirror. . . and a red curtain. Pushing past the curtain—what had happened next? . . . She dimly recollected having descended more stairs—having found herself once again in the hall. . . It was all frightfully obscure and dark!

In the act of reconstructing her experience she paused frequently. So deep was her abstraction that she was already standing quietly in the very ante-room she had recalled, before she was fully conscious that she had reached it. She looked up with a sudden start, and gave a single rapid, comprehensive glance around the apartment. The three doors were there—closed and forbidding, as before. The coloured light of the hall had given the place to a sort of grey twilight. . .

It was all perfectly real to her senses, yet she had a disquieting feeling that she was wandering in a dream-house, where anything might happen. The excitement which had so far sustained her now began to ebb, and she grew frightened. She had no intention of retreating, but she liked the look of those doors less than ever. How she had plucked up courage to open one of them on the last occasion, she could not conceive. . . It had been the left-hand one. As it was useless to repeat that experience, she ought really now to try the middle door—if only she could bring herself to do so. The other, on the right, she dismissed with a little emphatic shiver. Its appearance *scared* her. She did not know why, but merely to be standing in front of it was formidable. She had an idea all the time that it was on the point of swinging solemnly open.

The headache had departed, but her nerves were in a low condition. She kept starting; her heart was hammering away; flush after flush came to her cheeks. Then a sudden panic possessed her. She was sure that that awful door was about to open. She imagined that something was waiting just behind it, preparing to glide out, to intercept her from the stairs. Hardly knowing what she did, she clutched the handle of the middle door. . . It opened. She passed in quickly and breathlessly, and hurriedly closed it again from within.

She stood in a small, wainscoted room, unfurnished except for a carved wooden couch that was against the further wall. The floor was bare, and the walls were undecorated. The apartment was duskily lighted from overhead, since not a single side-window existed.

Notwithstanding its emptiness, there was an atmosphere of stately opulence in the little chamber, which could only be accounted for by the exquisiteness of its dark, naked timber. Merely to be in it impressed her with a sense of personal dignity; it was like entering the private cabinet of a nobleman. . . She fancied that the presence of that solitary couch seemed to point to the room's being primarily intended as a place for intimate meetings. . . though that would be queer, too! . . .

She sat down, but in an erect attitude and without relaxing her muscles. She prepared herself to spring up suddenly again, if need were. In fact, she felt far from easy in her mind. To be sitting alone in that mysterious room, behind a closed door, which might at any minute be opened—the situation was not precisely tranquillising. . . What was she waiting for, and why did she not retire, since she had seen all there was to see? She asked herself the question, and found no satisfactory reason for remaining, but it was as if she were in a state of enchantment—she continued sitting, watching the door with nervous anxiety. Her sensitive fingers were playing time along the long, delicate scarf she wore round her neck. She dared not acknowledge to herself that she was *waiting* for that door to open, and yet perhaps she was.

She uttered a faint cry, and half-rose from the couch. The door was opening. . . Her terrified eyes met those of Judge!

She got up altogether, and stumbled towards him. Judge closed the door behind him quickly and quietly; then, coming up to her, he supported her with his arm to the couch, and both sat down. Isbel could not stare at him enough. He seemed younger, and different. It might have been the effect of the dim light, but it was too remarkable not to be noticed.

"How have you got here?" she asked, as soon as she could command her tongue.

He did not reply immediately, but continued gazing at her with a sort of stern kindness. His face was different. It was less sallow, less respectable, more powerful and energetic. . . and always *younger*. He looked no more that five-and forty.

"I've come straight from the East Room," he said at last. "I mustn't stop—the others are expecting me back. I left them in the drawing-room, while I returned to lock the East Room and bring away the key. I had forgotten to do so. When I got there—a minute ago—I saw the stairs, and here I am."

"But where are we?"

"In a strange place, I fear. I can't conceive how *you* have found your way up."

"I came up from the hall. . . What is that third door?"

"I've never ventured to enter. Perhaps someother time we will try it together. We haven't leisure now."

Isbel turned pale, and removed herself a little away from him.

"That's a strange thing to say. You know it's impossible."

"How do you regard this meeting, then?" He eyed her gravely.

"As accidental. . . Tell me—is this really a part of the house, or are we dreaming?"

"Possibly neither. I've been here many times in former years, and I'm still no wiser than on the first occasion. You may not be aware that in ten minutes' time neither of us will remember a single detail of this meeting?"

"I know. I also have been here before, though not in this room."

"Then you have been deceiving me?"

"By force of necessity."

"Yes, you could not have acted differently. Those stairs have an irresistible attraction. I know the feeling, and how everything else has to give way."

Isbel still toyed with her scarf. "Did you guess that I was practising a stratagem on you?"

"No, it didn't occur to me, although I did not altogether understand your anxiety to have the house."

"Now I've sunk hopelessly in your estimation?"

"No—but you have succeeded in depressing me. I dreamt of friendship, and I wake up to find it's nothing of the sort."

She looked at him with a strange smile.

"When you came in just now, and found me sitting here, what passed through your mind?"

"I was unaware that you were here as the result of a fixed purpose. I thought it was your first visit, and I presumed to imagine that fate had brought us together. Pardon my audacity."

"And why do you suppose that your friendship is a matter of such indifference to me?"

"Because you have used it as an instrument for your designs."

"It is *not* a matter of indifference to me," she said, in a very low voice. . . "As everything is to be forgotten so soon, there's no object in my concealing my true feelings. There is such a thing as honour. I am to marry another man, and all my love is for him. But though I can't and mustn't love you, you have already influenced my life very strongly, and I feel that you will go on doing so more and more. I don't wish our friendship to die away—on the contrary, I wish it to become richer and more intimate. I've deceived you in other things, but not in that."

Judge's manner appeared curiously humble. "If I have had some influence on your life, you have inspired me to new life altogether. Before I met you, I was a lost man. I was wifeless and friendless. . . I don't think I could go on without your friendship. I'm willing to pay higher prices than the one you've exacted."

They looked at each other in silence for a minute.

"We shall understand each other better after this," said Isbel, softly. "Even if our minds forget, something in us will remember."

"Perhaps; but give me something to remember by."

After a moment's reflection, Isbel slowly unwound the silk scarf from her neck. "Take this, then!"

He glanced at her before accepting it. "Won't its absence be remarked?"

"It's mine to dispose of, I think. I'm not giving anything with it except respect and kindness."

Judge held out his hand, took the scarf, and, after carefully, almost reverently folding it into small compass, bestowed it in the breast-pocket of his coat.

"I shall guard it as the most precious of secrets. . . I have an idea that we shall meet here again."

She shook her head doubtfully. "It's a fearful place. I'm not sure that we have either of us done right to come here at all."

"Do you feel a worse woman for having spent these few minutes with me?"

"Oh, no—no! . . . Not worse, but, far, far better! I feel. . . it's impossible to describe. . ."

"Try!"

"I feel. . . just as if I'd had a *spiritual lesson. . .* It's foolish. . ."

"Let me interpret for you. Isn't it your feeling that during the short time we have spent here together we have been enabled temporarily to drop the mask of convention, and talk to each other more humanly and truthfully? Isn't this what you feel?"

"Yes, I think it is. . . The air here seems different. It's nobler, and there's a sort of music in it. . . If it hadn't been for this strange meeting, we should never have known each other so well. Perhaps not at all."

"Then we have done right to come here."

Isbel got up, and started walking about restlessly. Judge sat where he was, with a face of stone. Presently she stopped short in front of him, and demanded with quiet suddenness:

"What can be waiting for us in that other room?"

"We must find out—but not now. I must go now."

"But haven't you formed a guess?"

"I have somehow received the impression that this room and the left-hand one are merely *lobbies* to that other. If we are to experience anything, it will be there. All this is only preliminary."

"I think so, too," said Isbel. "But I should never find the courage to enter that room alone."

"We'll go together. The same fortune which has brought us face to face here this afternoon will provide us with an opportunity."

He got to his feet.

"So now we separate, in order to meet again?" asked Isbel.

"As strangers, unfortunately."

"No." She spoke with quiet dignity. "Hearts which have once met can never be strangers. I am sure we shall know each other."

They moved towards the door, and, as they did so, the same idea occurred for the first time to both.

"Surely we couldn't both have come up the same flight of stairs?" asked Isbel.

"I know of only one way up. We must have done."

"But I came up from the hall, and I only climbed to the height of one storey."

"We have to recognise, I fear, that physical properties here are different. I have plagued my head sufficiently over all that. I'm not disposed to worry about it any longer. . . We will go down together, but I think we shall lose sight of each other on the stairs."

They passed through the door, into the ante-room.

"Couldn't we put it to the test, by my taking your arm?" queried Isbel.

"Better not play with unknown forces, I think."

He bowed, and stood aside to allow her to precede him down the staircase.

Halfway down, she turned her head to see if he were still there following, but he had disappeared.

X

Blanche Speaks out

The hall was as she had left it, and her friends apparently had not yet returned. Her head was bewildered; she was unable at first to realise what had happened to her. She knew that a staircase had appeared to her, that she had climbed it some little time ago, and that it was only this minute that she had come down again. But the stairs had vanished, and her memory concerning the adventure was an utter blank. Pressing her hand to her hot forehead, she stared earnestly at the wall, in the effort to concentrate her will on that one task of recollection; but it was quite useless—the experience, whatever it was, had grazed her mind as lightly as a dream. . . Yet it had now happened to her twice, and it had happened to Mr. Judge as well, in years gone by. . .

She made up her mind to talk to that man on the subject. He was the only one to whom she *could* talk about it, and it was impossible to go on any longer hugging this awful secret in solitude. . . That would be the best. He might be angry at Marshall's breach of confidence, but perhaps it would be possible to contrive that that should not come out. She need not decide now. When she got home she would think about it all out carefully, weighing the affair in all its bearings. . .

Her watch told her that it was close upon half-past three. It was evident that she had been *somewhere* all that time. . . Then suddenly she realized the absence of her scarf. Uttering an exclamation of annoyance, she quickly cast her eyes around for the missing article, but it was nowhere visible in the hall, and she had not been in any other part of the house. She concluded that she must have dropped it out of doors—perhaps where they had picnicked in that field. She did not value the scarf highly, but it was vexing to lose it so stupidly. It would not take long to run there and back before the others came downstairs again.

Passing out of the hall-door, she retraced their route to the place where they had lunched, keeping a sharp watch for the bright, silken fabric, which ought to catch the eye quickly enough. She covered the whole distance, only stopping short at the little stream, but failed to see it anywhere. Then, recollecting that Blanche might possibly have picked it up and taken charge of it, she returned more quietly to the house.

The little distraction had at least one good result, it enabled her for a few minutes to forget that other thing, thereby permitting her nerves to tranquillise themselves, and in consequence she was now in a position to meet her friends again with tolerable coolness. On re-entering the hall she found them waiting for her; they seemed to have just come down.

Even before anyone spoke, Isbel was conscious of a changed atmosphere. An air of constraint hung over the little party, and for a moment she had a guilty feeling that this embarrassment was in some way connected with herself. No one remembered to inquire after the condition of her head.

Blanche addressed her with a cold smile: "We seem to be playing at hide-and-seek this afternoon. First Mr. Judge loses himself, and then you."

"I'm exceedingly sorry. I missed my scarf, and went outside to look for it. You haven't picked it up by any chance?"

"No."

"It doesn't matter, but it's gone."

"You haven't been upstairs, have you?"

"No—oh, no. Why?"

"You needn't look so startled—I only meant you had it round your neck when we went up. It was the last thing I saw."

"Surely not!" said Isbel, much puzzled.

"Were you in the hall all the time, up to the moment you missed it?"

"Yes."

Blanche shrugged her shoulders, and turned away.

"Mrs. Stokes must be mistaken, and you *must* have dropped it out of doors," suggested Judge. "I'll tell Priday to institute a thorough search for it. When found, I'll send it on."

"Thank you very much!"

Isbel kept stealing perplexed glances at Judge, and each time she did so she surprised him in the act of hastily averting his eyes from her. She could not imagine why they were regarding each other with such furtive interest. As far as she knew, nothing had changed in their relations since they had last spoken together, yet now it seemed as if they had a great deal to say to each other which they had somehow failed to discover at the time. She wondered how she could get to speak to him again.

"How did Mr. Judge contrive to get lost, then?" she inquired of Roger, who appeared the most approachable of the trio.

"With perfect ease. Blanche and I were wandering about the premises, like Adam and Eve turned out of Eden, for the space of half an hour."

"I can only repeat my apologies," said Judge rather stiffly. "I admit it was a most unpardonable breach of courtesy."

Isbel looked from one to another. "How did it come about, then?"

"The explanation is not very much to my credit, Miss Loment, but I fear I have no right to stand on dignity. We had come downstairs from the top storey, after visiting the East Room, and were about to enter the drawing-room, when I suddenly remembered that I had omitted to lock that other room again—which is to break my own rule. Mrs. Stokes was kind enough to allow me a couple of minutes' leave of absence to attend to the business. . ."

"Which Mr. Judge promptly extended to half an hour," said Blanche, with her back still turned.

"Why, what happened?"

"A somewhat absurd accident, Miss Loment. Whether it was the hot sun, or the wine, I don't know, but I fell asleep upstairs."

"How funny!" Isbel began to laugh.

Blanche swung round. "But the funniest thing was that when we went upstairs to look for him he was nowhere to be found."

"I repeat, Mrs. Stokes—because you looked in the wrong place. I was in one of the servants' rooms. I recollected having seen a window left open, and went along to shut it."

"Quite a chapter of accidents!" said Isbel. "However, the main thing is we're all happily assembled again, safe and sound, after our various adventures. Did you see anything interesting, Roger?"

"Much. The house is a veritable *pot-pourri* of styles and centuries. I have counted three distinct periods, and perhaps there are more."

Judge entered the conversation with a visible effort. "This hall is one, the main body of the house is another, but what is the third?"

"Why, the East Room. There's old, old, very old work there, unless I'm crassly ignorant. One of the rafters of the ceiling is carved with runes. *That* was placed there by no Elizabethan hand."

"You said nothing about this at the time?"

"I had no audience, my dear proprietor. My lady-wife was gazing around for ghosts, while you were deep in abstract thought, and did not once remove your eyes from the blank wall they chanced to alight on."

"But what would be the object of this carving?" demanded Isbel hurriedly.

"Doubtless a magic formula employed by our heathen Saxon forefathers to prevent the goblins from riding the roof—a favourite supernatural pastime of the olden days. Were I Judge, I would fain remove the timber and send it to our authorities to be deciphered."

"Perhaps I will," said Judge.

Isbel did not listen to Roger very attentively: she was cogitating Judge's story. She did not believe that he had spoken the truth. A quite different explanation of his disappearance had dawned on her, and with Isbel's intuitions from dawn to full day was but a flash. On his return to the East Room, he had seen that the staircase again which he had seen so many times before. He had ascended it, and—her heart beat rapidly—they two had met *up there*! . . . That was why they had been glancing at each other so strangely. . . She was as sure of it all as if she had heard it from his own mouth.

She turned aside in sick excitement.

"We'd better get home," remarked Blanche coldly. "It's nearly four, and I shan't be sorry for some tea."

Judge glanced at her rather anxiously "Would you prefer to stop somewhere en route?"

"We'll get home, I think."

As there was nothing to wait for, they at once left the hall. The girls went in front, but as soon as they were outside Blanche accompanied her husband to the car, leaving the others on the doorstep while Judge prepared to lock up.

"I'm coming over to Worthing tomorrow, to see you," murmured Isbel, standing straight up, facing the door and Judge.

Without changing countenance or so much as looking at her, he bent down to insert the key in the hole.

"Certainly, Miss Loment."

"I'll come over by train in the morning. Can you meet me on the front, as if by accident? Do you know a train?"

"There's the 10.40 from Hove."

"That will do. Please don't say a word to anyone."

Without waiting for his response, she hastened to join her friends. The two girls resumed their wraps, and got into the back seat. Judge took his place behind the wheel, and lastly Roger climbed in. After a little preliminary backing, they made a clear start down the drive.

At the lodge-gate they stopped for a minute, while Mrs. Priday called her husband out, in obedience to Judge's request. The head gardener was in the middle of tea, and his mouth was still busily engaged, in spite of his efforts to empty it.

"Priday," said his master, leaning out of the car towards him, "one of the ladies has lost a scarf somewhere on the grounds. It might be as far away as the stream by Moss's Wood. Have a good look round for it—today. It must be found."

"Colour, sir?"

Judge mutely transferred the inquiry to Isbel.

"*Vieux rose.* A long silk scarf."

"Pink, Priday. See to it at once. Good afternoon!"

BLANCHE PAID A VISIT TO Isbel's room that evening, during the dressing hour before dinner. Isbel, fully gowned, was sitting on a sofa, reading a magazine. Blanche had on the frock which she had worn on the occasion of the dinner-party; she refused to sit down, and altogether seemed rather unusual in her manner. Isbel, being in a highly sensitive mood, detected the presence of feminine electricity at once; she quietly set down her paper beside her, feeling more apprehension than she cared to admit to herself.

"What's the matter, Blanche?"

"Nothing. I've just looked in."

"I thought perhaps you wanted to say something. . . Well, have you enjoyed your day?"

"Oh, I expect so. Have you?"

"Yes—but I'm vexed about the scarf."

Blanche pointed her toes together and gazed down at the carpet. "Is it worth worrying about?"

"I hate losing things."

There was a pause.

"I know where it is—if that's any help to you," said Blanche quietly.

"You do? . . . Why, where is it?"

Her friend slowly lifted her eyes, until they stopped on Isbel's face. "In Judge's breast-pocket."

Isbel jumped up, then sat down again.

"*What!*"

"That's where it *was,* dear, at any rate, for I saw it there—peeping out."

"Oh, absurd! . . . What on earth should he be doing with my scarf?"

"I wonder you don't rather ask how it comes to be in his possession. You didn't give it to him, I presume?"

"I decidedly didn't. I'm not in the habit of giving articles of clothing to men."

Blanche pursed her lips for a second or two. . . "You certainly were wearing it when we went upstairs. You never came upstairs at all, and Judge never went downstairs. Yet the next time we meet him, it has become mysteriously transferred to his pocket. He hadn't even taken common precautions to hide it. . . Somewhat puzzling, don't you think?"

Danger signals appeared suddenly on Isbel's cheeks.

"You infer. . . ?"

"Nothing, dearest. But if you're speaking the truth—as I hope, for your own sake, you are—then that man isn't. In any case, he isn't. A girl's scarf doesn't float upstairs and find its way into a man's pocket of its own sweet will."

"Most likely it wasn't my scarf at all."

"My dear child, whatever else I don't know, I do know the contents of your wardrobe. You might put Roger off with that suggestion, but not me. It *was* your scarf."

Isbel bit her lip, and stared at the carpet beneath her.

"Then all I can say is, he must be pretty far gone. He has no right to it, and I don't know in the least what he's doing with it. Perhaps it's a form of mania with him."

"Yes—but you *won't* see the point. How did he get hold of it?"

"I expect after he had made his escape from you he slipped quietly down the servants' staircase and got into the hall that way. Finding me asleep, he appropriated the scarf. I can't think of any other solution."

"He *may* be a lunatic, of course," said Blanche, in her driest tone.

"Thanks! I quite understand what you're driving at all along."

Blanche said nothing. Isbel, after waiting in vain for her to speak, uttered a high, metallic laugh.

"Oh, I admit the evidence is overwhelmingly damning against both of us. You might as well be honest about it."

"For heaven's sake don't take up that tone! You must see for yourself how it compromises you. Instead of losing your temper, you had much better set about recovering your property. If I've seen it, somebody else may."

"From which I assume that you don't propose to acquaint the others with the details of this romantic affair?"

"I'm not a sneak. You ought to know me better than that."

Isbel gnawed away at her finger-nails.

"I came here to try and help you," went on Blanche. "It's not very encouraging to find myself treated as an interfering busybody."

"Oh, don't imagine I'm not grateful to you. It isn't everyone who would undertake such an unpalatable duty—I quite see that. . . Perhaps I should have been even more grateful to you for a little loyal backing up, but I see your point of view perfectly. I've no right to expect other people to behave as quixotically as I should have done under similar circumstances. Every woman must act according to her nature."

"It will be time enough to show sympathy when I know it's wanted."

"And deserved. Don't spare me, I beg."

Blanche sat down slowly on the sofa. After a minute she impulsively seized her friend's hand.

"Billy, swear there's nothing between you and that man, and I'll believe you. I don't think you could tell me a direct lie. Up to the present we've always shared each other's secrets."

"I do swear that I haven't the faintest notion how that scarf got out of my possession, or into his. I'm as utterly mystified as you are."

"Sure?"

"Quite sure," said Isbel, colouring and smiling.

"Very well; that's all I wanted to hear. As long as it's all right on your side, *his* conduct is of quite secondary importance. I'm more relieved than I can tell you. . . But you'll have to get it back, by fair means or foul."

"I'll think it over tonight in bed."

Blanche gazed at her steadily, still holding her hand.

"If I were you, I should drop the acquaintance altogether. You won't derive much good from a man like that."

"You mean, give up the idea of his house?"

"There are plenty of other houses. Have you told your aunt yet about his change of decision?"

"No."

"That's good. Don't. . . Dash a line off to Judge to say it's all over. And you can mention about the scarf at the same time. Say you understand it's in his possession, and beg him to return it at once. . . You could almost do it now, before dinner."

DAVID LINDSAY

"No, there isn't time," replied Isbel. And she found no time the whole of the evening.

In bed, the same night, she tossed for hours, tormenting her brain over the events of the day. As often as she had satisfactorily assured herself of the impossibility of her having given that scarf personally to Judge, the whole problem would break open again, like a badly-bandaged wound, and she would find herself once more searching in vain in all directions for some escape from the necessity of accepting this awful, unthinkable hypothesis.

Her thoughts travelled round and round in circles, and relief came to her at last only in absolute physical exhaustion.

XI

Isbel Visits Worthing

I mmediately after the departure of Blanche and Roger next morning, Isbel—attired in an old, though still serviceable, tweed walking costume, with stout, low-heeled shoes—announced her intention of taking a long tramp on the Downs by herself; she might, or might not, be back for lunch. It was the only programme she could think of in which her aunt would be certain not to offer to participate. Mrs. Moor, of course, raised some half-hearted objections—that was more in the nature of a ritual between the two ladies—but in the end Isbel got her way, and before ten o'clock she was out of the hotel. Not en route to the Downs, however. At the top of Preston Street she caught a bus to Hove Station, and, on arriving there, purchased a ticket to Worthing.

The train was a little overdue. Not many people were travelling, and she was able to secure an empty first-class compartment. Her first action was to fling down both windows for the atmosphere was suffocating close; it was one of those heavy, sluggish, overcast, depressing mornings which are the sure forerunners of steady rain. As they ran into Worthing, a few spots already began to gather on the left-hand side windows.

She found Judge waiting for her at the Parade end of South Street. He was smartly clad, had his hands behind him, and was gazing idly, yet with dignity, at the outside shelves of a book-dealer's shop. No one could have guessed from his manner that he was there by appointment. When she touched him lightly on the arm, his start of surprise nearly deceived herself into imagining that the meeting was accidental; but then she remembered her own caution to him.

"I *am* the one you're waiting for, I hope?" she asked, with a smile.

He replaced his hat. "I would have come to the station, but your instructions were definite."

"Then let's get on to the front. It's going to rain, isn't it?"

"I fear so—and you have no protection."

"I've nothing on to spoil."

They crossed the road to the Parade, and started to walk in the direction of the Burlington. There were a few people abroad, and certainly no one she knew, yet the mere fact that she was in a strange

DAVID LINDSAY

town, strolling with a strange man, had a peculiarly exciting effect upon her nerves. Everyone they passed seemed to be regarding her with suspicion.

"You didn't mind meeting me here this morning, Mr. Judge?"

"Just the reverse, Miss Loment. I regard it as a great honour."

"It's nothing very dreadful. I just wanted to talk things over."

"I quite understand." But he looked rather puzzled.

She waited till some approaching women had met and passed. "First of all, Mr. Judge—did you find my scarf?"

"Yes; it's in my pocket, and you shall have it when we separate. I've made a small parcel of it."

"Where was it found, then?"

He hesitated. "In a very queer resting-place, I'm afraid. On getting home last evening I found it reposing neatly folded in my breast-pocket."

"I see."

"Doubtless a practical joke on someone's part—a kind of joke, I must admit, I don't much care about."

"You mean Roger, I suppose? I don't think he would have done it. Couldn't you have placed it there yourself in a fit of abstraction?"

"No, that is entirely out of the question. I think we must call it a joke."

There was an interval of silence, and then she turned to him quietly: "Mr. Judge. . ."

"Yes, Miss Loment?"

"When you disappeared yesterday afternoon, where were you?"

"Surely I have explained that?"

"I don't blame you for giving an untrue account of your movements, because, of course, you had to say something. But you'll tell me the truth now, won't you?"

"But, really! . . ."

"You did go up those stairs, didn't you?"

Judge gave her a swift sidelong glance. "What stairs?"

"That strange staircase leading out of the East Room."

"Mr. Marshall Stokes told you, then?"

"Please leave him out of it. My information is first-hand."

It now came on to rain more sharply, and they were forced to take refuge in an adjacent shelter, which luckily proved to be vacant. They sat facing the sea. Judge rested both hands on his gold-headed stick, and stared straight before him.

"Yet I distinctly gathered that you have never personally visited that room, Miss Loment?"

"Nor have I. Your house has more mysteries than you are aware of, Mr. Judge. The hall also has its staircase."

"What staircase?" He frowned. "I don't quite know how to take this."

"Not only have I seen it with my own eyes, but I have twice set foot on it—once being yesterday afternoon. I want you to believe that I am being quite serious, and not fabricating in the least."

"Yesterday afternoon?"

"Five minutes after you had all gone upstairs."

"Could you describe them—those stairs?"

"The were plain, narrow, wooden stairs, going up through an opening in the wall; no handrail. The top was out of sight."

"This is indeed extraordinary! Can you tell me your experience?"

"No; for I remember nothing of it. But I went up them and came down again."

There was a long pause, during which Judge frequently cleared his throat.

"I must believe you, Miss Loment, and yet. . . And this was the second occasion, you tell me? Were you by yourself the first time as well?"

"Yes."

"I can't doubt your word; the same thing has happened to me more than a few times. Astonishing as your statement is, Miss Loment, in a sense I'm relieved by it. I may as well confess it—I have sometimes been alarmed for my reason. The stable laws of Nature are the foundation of the whole of our experience, and when once in a while we seem to see them no longer valid, it is inevitable that we should prefer to suspect our understanding."

"Then you did go up yesterday?"

"Yes, I did go up."

"And remember nothing?"

"Nothing whatever."

"Nothing that strikes you?"

"Might not we have *met* in that upper part of the house?"

Judge looked up quickly. "What makes you think that?"

"You don't realise that it might explain my scarf's being in your possession?" she asked in a very low voice.

"Your scarf?"

"Don't be in a hurry. Think it over for a minute, Mr. Judge. It's important."

"I cannot see how our meeting there, or anywhere else, would account for your scarf's being in my pocket."

"If you cannot see, I cannot help you."

"I am not a thief, and why should such a gift by made?"

"But perhaps it *was* made."

"I cannot imagine what you mean," said Judge, turning pale.

Isbel cast uneasy glances around her. She drew a little closer to him, re-arranging her skirt with nervous impatience.

"That's the another thing I wanted to talk about, Mr. Judge. I don't know how we really stand towards each other. . . Of course we're *friends. . .* Since yesterday, our relationship has somehow seemed to me very undefined. It has been worrying me."

"I think I understand what you mean."

"Is it our experience in common, or is it something else? Do try and help me. It's frightfully difficult for me to speak of all this."

"But is it necessary to, Miss Loment? As you say, we are friends. Perhaps if we show ourselves too curious, we shall merely be robbing ourselves of what we already possess."

"Oh, don't you see? If we don't know how we stand, we can't even be friends. How can I have a man for a friend whose feelings I have to guess at? . . . I believe I'm justified in asking you, I don't require you to commit yourself in anyway, and whatever you tell me, I shan't take advantage of it—but I think I ought to know just how it stands with you."

Judge kept closing and opening his hand agitatedly.

"We are really carrying the conversation too far, Miss Loment. You must see that you and I have no right whatever to discuss feelings."

"You don't or won't understand. If you have feelings which refer to me, they are my property, and I have a perfect right to know what they are." Her voice quietened. "I *must* ask you to tell me. . . Do you regard me. . . in any special manner? Or. . . Can't you see how awkwardly I am situated till I know how. . . we stand to each other?" she concluded weakly.

"We are good friends, Miss Loment, and nothing more."

"So you persist in setting up this icy barrier? But how can we go on meeting each other, if our heads are to remain full of unsatisfied fancies and suspicions? . . . I promise you one thing, Mr. Judge—if you decline to be my real friend, you shan't be my friend at all. I shall never want to see you again after this."

"I shall be sorry for that, but if everything is to finish so suddenly, at least I prefer that it shall not be owing to an act of egregious folly on my part. Since I don't possess the advantages of a younger man, I daren't imitate the rashness of one."

"But what are you afraid of? I can scarcely punish you for obeying me. Whatever you tell me, I promise you it shan't bring our friendship to a close. Nothing will be changed, except for the better. Won't you speak now?"

"I cannot."

She paled, and began to tap the asphalt paving with her foot. "You can hardly refuse to answer a direct question. Am I anything to you at all, Mr. Judge?"

"Perhaps you are a very great deal, but the point is, I can be nothing to you."

"You mean exactly that?"

"Yes. I have a higher regard for you, Miss Loment, than for any other living woman."

"But what is implied by a very high regard?" She could scarcely breathe the words out.

"There is a special term for that feeling but I am not permitted to pronounce it."

"Do I understand you correctly?" she asked, nearly inaudibly.

Judge made no reply.

After a long silence, Isbel gave a spasmodic, wavering sigh.

"Shall I take my scarf now? There's no one to see."

He produced a small brown paper packet from his pocket, and passed it over to her. She kept turning it in her hand, with a sort of weary indifference.

"What are we to do about it? You know we must find out how it came to be in your possession. I cannot go there again, but you can."

"If you wish me to. But of what use is it, if I am to remember nothing?"

"Could you not take pencil and paper?"

"That's an idea, and I can't conceive why it has never occurred to me before. Very well, then; I will run over."

"This afternoon. But how shall I communicate the result to you?"

"I don't wish you either to write or call, Mr. Judge. Couldn't you manage to come over to Brighton tomorrow afternoon, and see me somewhere?"

DAVID LINDSAY

"I *must* manage it. Where shall it be, and at what time?"

"My aunt always takes her rest in the afternoon, Let's say three o'clock—at the Hove, I think; there are fewer people there to bother one. You know the Baths, facing the sea?"

"Yes."

"Outside there, then. You see the importance of this to both of us, don't you?"

"My only motive in the business is to re-assure your mind. I draw no anticipations from the result."

Isbel gave him a keen glance. "Yet after what you have said, it can't be a matter of indifference to you."

"Candidly, Miss Loment, I don't wish for a result. I want our friendship to continue, and that will be impossible if. . . I desire nothing more than that we shall settle down again into the old pleasant state. I feel confident that you will find we have foolishly allowed our imaginations to run away with us over this matter."

They had both risen to their feet, but a heavier shower at that moment coming on, they were compelled to seat themselves again. Isbel turned her head away, and started fingering her hair.

"By the way," she announced suddenly, "I haven't mentioned your decision about the house yet to my aunt, so you had better not, either."

"Just as well not to I'm not sure at all, after this, that Runhill will make a suitable residence for you."

"For all that, I may keep you to your word. However, we won't do anything in a hurry. . . That woman will spoil her furs, if she's not careful."

She referred to an elegantly-garbed lady who was bearing down on their shelter from the west. She was obviously flurried by the distressing rain, as only a woman is flurried; but her action remained perfectly graceful and fascinating to watch, while she carried her furs and velvets as though they were a part of herself. Though tall and slender, it was evident even at that distance that she had long since finished with girlhood, but Isbel was unable as yet to distinguish her features. Judge happened to be sitting on her other side, so she failed to notice his embarrassment.

"It's an acquaintance of mine," he brought out somewhat quickly. "That is, she is staying at the same hotel. A Mrs. Richborough—a widow."

"Charming!" responded Isbel vaguely. "I can't see her face. Is she pretty?"

"More distinguished-looking than pretty. A most interesting woman to talk to—which is as far as my acquaintance extends. A keen spiritualist."

"Yes—I can see now. She's got one of those white, peaky faces. Is she well-off?"

"I really can't say. She has fashionable clothes and jewels. I am merely on nodding terms with her."

"She seems to be coming here. I think I'll go."

"No—don't, please, Miss Loment! It will look too marked. I'll just introduce you and you can take your departure immediately."

Isbel bent her mouth into a scornful little smile. "As you please. It's rather bad luck, but, anyway, she won't know me from Eve. . . Do tell me a train back. I expect you have a time-table."

He had, and produced it for consultation at once. While he was hurriedly turning over the leaves, Mrs. Richborough advanced upon them with a quickened step and a sudden smile of recognition—but, somehow, Isbel had a suspicion that the meeting was not quite so unpremeditated. All her poses were so accurately graceful and studied that the latter wondered if, by any chance, she could be a mannequin on holiday; her heels were perfect stilts. The face, however, when she came close up, was a good thirty-six or seven, and was not even decently pretty for that age. It was long, thin, and pale, with high cheek-bones and a fixed, insolent smile, which expressed nothing at all except pretension. But it was very beautifully made-up—so much so that it almost required another woman to see that it had been touched at all. Her whole toilette, from clothes to perfume, was based on an appeal to sex, and, men being such crude animals, Isbel thought that it was quite possible she might still pick up an occasional victim here or there. . . She glanced down at her own shabby tweeds, and smiled ironically.

"May I come in out of the weather? What a delightfully unexpected meeting!" Mrs. Richborough, without waiting for permission, stepped under the shelter and shook out her muff.

Judge, still holding the open time-table in his hand, rose with a courteous smile and removed his hat; he continued standing.

"It is indeed a pleasant surprise! But aren't you terribly wet?"

"A little. . . Am I intruding?" Her voice was quiet, sweet almost to lusciousness, and very leisurely. Each word was produced with a distinctness nearly theatrical, but at the conclusion of all her periods she had the strange trick of dropping to a whisper.

"Not in the least," replied Judge. "We're cast up here by the rain, and very thankful to see a new face. This is a friend of mine. . . Miss Loment—Mrs. Richborough. . . I'm just in the act of looking up a train for Miss Loment, if you'll pardon me a minute."

Mrs. Richborough sank lightly down next to Isbel.

"You aren't a Worthing resident, then?"

"Oh, no. Do I look like one?"

"I hardly know how one distinguishes them by appearance. Then you come from. . . ?"

"From Brighton. Why?"

The widow laughed. "I really can't say why I'm asking. Why does one ask these things? So Mr. Judge is in Fortune's good graces this morning. Was yours accidental, too?"

"My what? . . . I fear the rain won't have done your beautiful furs much good."

"Isn't it perfectly distressing? And I so hoped it was to be fine. You have been sensible, at any rate."

"You mean my get-up? Oh, I put these on specially to come over here."

Mrs. Richborough glanced at the little parcel on Isbel's lap. "Surely you didn't bring lunch with you?"

"Oh, no; I'm only here on business."

Judge at last succeeded in finding a train. It would convey her to Brighton in time for luncheon, but she would have to start for the station at once, and lose no time on the way.

Mrs. Richborough held out her hand. "I hope we shall resume the acquaintance under more propitious circumstances."

Isbel returned the slightest and coldest of bows, deliberately overlooking the hand.

"No, don't trouble to come with me, Mr. Judge," she said, touching his fingers, with a smile. "People who run for trains aren't very good company, and I know the way quite well."

And she immediately set off through the rain in the direction of the railway station.

XII

Mrs. Richborough's Errand

Wednesday afternoon turned out cold and fine, with a watery sun. Isbel arrived at the rendezvous at a few minutes before the appointed time, but Judge was not yet there.

She was fashionably but inconspicuously dressed in a dark serge costume, with skunk furs; at the back of her mind was the desire to correct any possible wrong impression caused by her unfortunately-chosen attire of yesterday. After pacing up and down the parade in front of the Baths for a good while, however, with carefully assumed nonchalance, she began to fear that her forethought would be wasted; no one even distantly resembling Judge was in sight.

Her feelings passed from disappointment to impatience, and thence to anger, by the gradations which familiar to everyone who has ever been kept waiting. At a quarter past three she decided that it was inconsistent with her dignity as a woman to stay for his good pleasure any longer. . . yet five minutes later she had still not dragged herself away from the spot. . .

She was really going, when she caught sight of a familiar person approaching her—a surprising vision, which caused her to catch her breath and turn rather pale. It was Mrs. Richborough. She was mincing along the parade, without any great appearance of haste, from the direction of Brighton. Her furs were still very much in evidence, but they were different from those she had worn yesterday, being even heavier and more expensive-looking; she had on a smart black velvet toque, ornamented with a single paradise feather, and was wearing quite new white gloves. Isbel feared that her presence there was directly connected with Judge's absence; she felt wretchedly sure that something must have happened to him. Without standing on pretence, she hurried to meet the widow.

They met, and lightly touched hands—Mrs. Richborough with a correct smile, but Isbel too worried to think of observances.

"I suppose you come from Mr. Judge?" she demanded, at once.

"I do, and I'm frightfully sorry I couldn't get here before, for I know what girls are when they're disappointed. . . but really—I'm so out of breath with running here. . . you *will* excuse me, won't you? The trains, as usual, are running just at the wrong time. . . You see how distressed I am with hurrying."

"Never mind. Why couldn't he come himself?"

"He's unwell. . . No—not badly. A chill on the liver, or something of the kind. Of course, we know he's not as young as he was. He *wanted* to come, but I wouldn't hear of it. rather than that he should risk more serious complications, I offered to act as messenger myself. . . Shall we sit down?"

"You're sure it's nothing serious?"

"Oh, my dear! . . . It's only a cold. He'll be all right tomorrow again."

They sat down side by side on one of the public seats. Mrs. Richborough made a feint of recovering her breath, which Isbel did not condescend to notice.

"Have you brought a note from him, or is it a verbal message?"

"It's a letter, my dear. I'm going to find it in a minute." She opened her hand-bag, and peered into it with provoking leisureliness. . . "Do you know, I feel quite an *intrigante*. Of course, it isn't a romance, but I've been amusing myself all the way here by imagining it really to be one. I've a fearfully romantic disposition."

"Oh, it's only about his house, which my aunt proposes to buy."

"How disillusioning! . . . So you act as her business manager?"

"I help her sometimes. Is that the note?"

"It's a little crumpled, but otherwise quite intact."

Isbel turned the large, square envelope over in her hand; it was unaddressed, but sealed with yellow wax. Contact with Mrs. Richborough's scent-sachet in her bag had invested it with a heavy feminine odour. She examined the sealing-wax more closely than was altogether courteous.

"Does he want me to read it now, and return an answer?"

"He *is* rather expecting one, I fancy. Don't study me, my dear—I shan't look."

Isbel still fingered the envelope. "You're not in his confidence, naturally?"

"That's quite a horrid question!" The widow's voice remained soft, but her eye was hard and insolent. "I'm afraid we haven't arrived at that stage of intimacy yet."

"I didn't know."

She hesitated no longer, but at once broke open the envelope. Her companion discreetly bent down to lift and minutely inspect the hem of her skirt; she allowed it to fall again gracefully, and then produced from her bag a little silver mirror, in which she critically scrutinised her reflected features.

In addition to a letter, there was something wrapped in white paper, and this Isbel opened first. It proved to be a hairpin. She gazed at in blank astonishment, and then hurriedly thrust it back inside the envelope, before Mrs. Richborough should see. The letter itself was in Judge's firm, precise hand-writing, and ran as follows:

My dear Miss Loment

"I am not quite the thing today, so please forgive my non-attendance. Mrs. R. has very kindly offered to run over to see you and bring you this letter with enclosure. The latter was picked up—you know where. The pencil-note I brought back with me from the same place related, I am reluctant to inform you, only to my own personal feelings, and I have taken the liberty to destroy it; but I am afraid that your hypothesis is, after all, correct. If you are able to identify the article enclosed, we must regard the evident as conclusive.

"I now propose that we shall go over there tomorrow (Thursday) *together*. Mrs. R. has kindly volunteered to accompany us, and, if you think well of the proposition, perhaps you will fix up things with her. She knows nothing of the affair in question. Very probably I have no right to ask you to come, and I do not do so on my own account—which I believe you understand. But I know what anxiety the whole business is causing you, and *must* cause you so I thought it only fair that the opportunity should be placed within your reach, should you desire to avail yourself of it. If you are unable to arrange for tomorrow, perhaps you could give Mrs. R. another date?

"It is unnecessary to impress on you the desirability of destroying this letter at the earliest moment.

Very sincerely yours
H.J.

Isbel read through the missive twice, then returned it thoughtfully to the envelope and placed the latter in her hand-bag.

"Thanks, Mrs. Richborough!"

The widow, who was in the act of adjusting her veil, turned about with a quick, impulsive smile.

"Everything satisfactory, my dear?"

"As regards the main business—yes. But he says something about our all going over to Runhill Court tomorrow. . ."

"Do let's! I'm positively dying to see that place."

"Why?"

"I dote on these ancient family houses. I don't know why. I'm more than a little mediumistic—that may be one reason."

"If you're so keen, you needn't wait for me, I suppose."

Mrs. Richborough's smile faded. "I suppose not, if I could find another woman. Unluckily, I know nobody in this part of the world. My own set happens to be up North."

"Is there no one at the hotel?"

"I'm just a little exclusive, I fear. . . Why shouldn't you come, my dear? What are you afraid of?"

"You don't know, of course—I've already seen that place three times. There are limits to one's enthusiasm. . . I don't think I'll come, thanks!"

"This is truly unexpected. Most girls would be charmed at the prospect of another pleasure-party."

"The only pleasure I can see in it is the pleasure of your society, Mrs. Richborough. Of course, that is a great inducement."

"No, don't be horride, my dear. Let me put it in a different form. Perhaps you're not keen on coming; but do it to please Mr. Judge. The poor man's so proud of his house, and so delighted—so almost childishly delighted at the opportunity of exhibiting it to his friends. For some unknown reason, he chooses to set a very high value on my artistic opinion, and I have promised to tell him *honestly* exactly what I think of Runhill Court. . . And now, because you're afraid of being a little bored, you're going to dash all our plans to the ground."

Isbel laughed. "The long and short of it is I'm not wanted for my own sake, but only to act as chaperon to *you.*"

The widow, too laughed—so energetically that her long, white face became quite strange to look at.

"It sounds rather weird for an unmarried girl to chaperon an experienced widow, but you know, my dear, two women can always go where one can't. After all, I have my reputation to lose, just as much as the youngest and most innocent of you. . . You *will* come now, won't you?"

"I'm still rather at sea, Mrs. Richborough. Is all this solicitude on your account, or Mr. Judge's?"

"On his—because I'm so sorry for him. The poor man is so lonely. He's lost his wife, he has no friends to speak of, and he lives all by himself in a seaside hotel, where he's surrounded by a set of entirely new faces everyday. We women ought to do what we can for him. I know he can't be precisely a congenial companion for a girl your age, but if you'll only act the good Samaritan and come with us I give you my solemn word of honour I'll take as much of his conversation off your hands as I can manage."

"Oh, I don't doubt that in the very least."

"Then you consent?"

"No, I refuse," said Isbel, dryly.

"It's too bad of you! . . . Won't you give a reason? I must tell him something."

"Tell him I don't care to. He'll understand. Tell him I don't care to go running about the country with total strangers. I don't like it, and my friends wouldn't like it. . . Thanks for coming over, Mrs. Richborough! There's nothing else you want to say, is there?" She prepared to get up.

"One little minute more, my dear. . . If you don't care about accompanying us, would your aunt, I wonder? You say she is negotiating for the house. Mr. Judge, of course, would bring his car for her."

"I'm afraid if he brought wild horses it wouldn't have the desired effect. She's a very difficult person to move."

"There's nothing like trying. If I were to walk back with you to your hotel, should I find her in?"

"She would be in, but whether she would be visible is quite another matter. I may as well tell you that her interest in Runhill Court is extremely thin at the moment, and as for Mr. Judge—merely to mention his name is like holding out a red cloak to a bull. . . She fancies he hasn't treated her with an excessive amount of consideration—and that's really why the negotiations are falling on me."

"There would be no harm in my trying, though. I think I *will* look in on my way to the station. It's the Hotel Gondy, isn't it? I fancy I once stayed there."

"You seem quite well posted," said Isbel, smiling with vexation. "Go, by all means, if you think it's at all likely to answer the purpose. Only, please don't bring my name into it—I particularly request that."

The widow shot her a malicious little glance.

"If it can *possibly* be avoided, my dear, it shall be. In any case, she shall hear nothing of the letter—I promise you that."

"I begin to see!"

"I can hardly do more, can I? If we aren't to be friends, you really can't expect me to fib for you. Be reasonable!"

"No, I really suppose I can't. . . The only thing that still puzzles me is why my humble society should be so much in request. Such red-hot zeal in the cause of sight-seeing strikes one as quite uncanny! Surely you can't have told me the whole story?"

"I believe we shall come to terms now. Do you know, my dear, you're ever so much cleverer than I gave you credit for at first." She bestowed on Isbel one of those disarming smiles which she ordinarily reserved for her male acquaintances. "As you're so direct with me, I'm going to be equally open with you. Runhill Court is notoriously haunted, and. . . I'm a spiritist. . . That explains everything at last, doesn't it?"

Isbel stared at her. "But is it notoriously haunted?"

"Perhaps 'haunted' is a rather misleading term. Shall we say *queer?* There's a corridor there which is quite celebrated throughout the length and breadth of the kingdom—in psychic circles, it goes without saying. You must know it, since you've been there so many times?"

"Oh, yes—but if that's all, it's not much."

"Not to you, my dear, for you take no interest in such matters, but to anyone who is interested in another world the smallest clue is deeply engrossing. Possibly you have never lost anyone who is very, very dear to you? I have."

"And that's the true reason why I'm to be forced to do something I don't want? Excuse my scepticism, Mrs. Richborough, but you've been rattling out different explanations at the rate of sixty miles an hour for the last ten minutes. I'm not sure whether there are more to come."

The widow threw her a hostile glance. "Such as what?"

"That's what I don't know, and what I am wondering."

"You seem to suggest a personal motive?"

"I suggest nothing at all, but it's very funny. . . How long have you really known Mr. Judge?"

"Exactly a fortnight tomorrow, my dear. You see, there's no question of intimacy between us."

"What is the extent of his fortune, really? I've never heard."

Mrs. Richborough showed her long, but beautifully white teeth, in a smile. "Has he one? He has that house, of course. . . I confess I've never heard whether he's rich or poor, and, to tell the truth, it doesn't worry me in the slightest. I'm afraid I'm a dreadfully unmercenary creature; I choose my friends for their distinction of character, and not at all for their money-bags. I've never had anything to do with money, and I hate the very mention of it."

"Then how do you contrive to live?" asked Isbel bluntly.

"Oh, one has an income, of course. . . still, one leaves all that to one's banker. The great art of living happily, my dear, is to cut your coat according to your stuff. . . Now, it's getting late—what about tomorrow?"

"I suppose I shall have to say 'Yes,' since you're so very persuasive."

"I felt sure you would relent eventually."

"On condition that the whole thing is kept quiet."

Mrs. Richborough reassured her with effusiveness.

"It had better be in the morning," said Isbel, cutting her short somewhat contemptuously.

"I was going to suggest it. I'm so glad you can fit in—I know how horribly tied you girls are. They call it a free country, yet a girl is a perfect slave to her little circle. . . Now, will you come over to Worthing by the same train as before? Come straight along to the Metropole, and ask for me. The car will be waiting, and we can start at once—just the three of us."

"How do you know that Mr. Judge will be sufficiently recovered to come?"

"Oh, he will be. There's nothing seriously wrong with him, my dear. I shall pack him off to bed early, and see that he gets a real goodnight's rest."

Isbel stood up. "He's evidently in good hands."

"Any woman would do that much for him. It would be abominable to leave him to the mercies of the hotel staff." Mrs. Richborough also ascended to the perpendicular position—a floating mass of soft furs. . . "You don't wish me to convey a personal message?"

"Oh, say I'm sorry he's unwell, and that the other matter is all right."

She extended her hand, which the widow hastened to grasp warmly. The latter even raised her veil and pushed her face forward, but this was too much for Isbel, who deliberately ignored the invitation. Mrs. Richborough, recognising her *faux pas*, made all speed to cover it up:

"I hear you're to be married, my dear?"

"Oh, yes. . . Who told you?"

"Mr. Judge *hinted* at it. . . I'm so glad!"

"Thanks! But I wish he'd leave my private affairs alone."

"He's so isolated, and had so little to talk about."

"He has no right to discuss *me.* I don't like it."

"My dear, it was only the shadow of a hint—perhaps not even that. Perhaps he said nothing at all, and it was merely my intuition. . . Well, then, goodbye till tomorrow. By the way, if you would care to dash off a few lines to him, I have paper and a fountain pen."

Isbel declined, thinking the offer rather strange. They separated, to go their respective ways.

Five minutes later, as she passed along the now nearly deserted parade towards the hotel, she whipped a hairpin out of her hair, and, halting for a moment, compared it carefully with that which Judge had sent her. They were identical in size and shape. . . She returned them both to her hair.

XIII

The Lunch at the Metropole

It had been raining heavily, but the sky was rapidly clearing and there were great tracts of blue everywhere as Isbel mounted the steps of the Metropole Hotel at Worthing shortly after noon on the following day. She had been unable to escape from her aunt in time to catch the earlier train, but to compensate for this she was free to spend the whole day as she pleased. By a lucky chance, Mrs. Moor was compelled to go up to town on business.

Judge was waiting in the porch. He grasped her hand warmly, preventing her apologies.

"It was very good of you to come at all, Miss Loment. As far as we are concerned, the time is of no importance. Mrs. Richborough will be here immediately."

Even as he spoke, the widow appeared. Her tall and lovely form was attired as usual in the rich, soft furs and velvets which she so much affected. She moved charmingly, and her gracefully swaying waist was that of a quite young woman, but Isbel no sooner saw the angular, witchlike face than her old feelings of repugnance and distrust returned.

As it was so late, an early lunch at the hotel was agreed upon, before starting. They passed into the restaurant. Here Isbel received an unpleasant shock. She recognised and was recognised by a girl acquaintance belonging to her particular set—Louie Lassells, who probably was more intimate with Blanche, Marshall, and the rest than with her own relations.

Louie was lunching with a couple of youngsters of the subaltern type; she seemed in the highest spirits, and champagne was already on the table. She pledged Isbel in a glass from the other side of the room. Presently she came over to her, her dark, bold, handsome, gypsy-like face looked very flushed and defiantly gay.

"So this is where you get to!" she began, throwing a single critical glance towards Mrs. Richborough and Judge.

"I'm not the only one, it appears," retaliated Isbel. She laid down her knife and fork, and looked up calmly. "You're having a high old time, obviously."

"Rather! We're making a day of it. Sorry I can't introduce you, but we're all here *incog*. I'm supposed to be in Regent Street at this blessed minute."

"Bravo! I'm supposed to be in Brighton. We'd better draw up a deed."

Louie laughed immoderately. "What shall we drink it in?" Her eye roved round the table. "What *are* you drinking? Only Burgundy? . . . I say. . ."—she bent to whisper—"you're not having much of a time, are you? Where did you dig them up?"

Mrs. Richborough unluckily overheard.

"Surely I know your face?" she remarked graciously to Louie, who still held on to the edge of the table. "Your name is just hovering on the tip of my tongue."

The girl smiled vaguely, without even looking at her. "One sees so many people. It's going to turn out a quite charming day, I think. . . Well, ta-ta, Isbel! No manner of use asking you to join us, of course?"

"You see, I can't."

Louie trod lightly back to her impatient squires, while Isbel watched with some amusement Mrs. Richborough's efforts to regain her composure.

"She seems a pleasant girl," remarked Judge.

"Is she a very close friend of yours?" inquired the widow of Isbel, returning, however, to her plate.

"We know each other fairly well."

"What an unfortunate coincidence that she should be lunching here today, of all days."

"Why?" asked Judge.

"Miss Loment rather wished to keep her visit private, I fancy. I'm afraid she is inclined to regard it in the light of an escapade."

"Is that really so, Miss Loment?"

"Naturally I have appearances to consider. However, it's no good crying over spilt milk if anyone splits, it won't be Louie."

"Quite sure?" asked Mrs. Richborough, with a smile which almost a sneer.

"I hope I can trust my own friends to behave with common decency."

Judge looked perplexed. "I hope you're not here against your will?"

"Why should I come, if I hadn't wanted to? I'm a free agent."

"Can't you grasp, Mr. Judge? *La tante terrible!* Miss Loment is experiencing the fearful joy of being out of school."

"Clever, but unsound, Mrs. Richborough. I was thinking more of public opinion."

"You think you are acting unwisely?" asked Judge, wrinkling his forehead.

"Oh, I know if there's any doubt about it the judgement won't be given in my favour. Lunching in a strange town, with quite unknown people, strikes me as being exactly calculated to lead to a lot of questions being asked. And we know that if a question is uncharitable, the answer to it won't be otherwise. Even if I were to plead altruistic motives, I'm afraid it wouldn't be of any avail."

"Does that imply you're here out of kindness?"

"Perhaps it comes to that in the end. The pleasure of a chaperon is always rather impersonal."

"Of a chaperon, Miss Loment?"

"Didn't you know? I'm chaperoning Mrs. Richborough. She made such a strong point of it that really I hadn't the heart to refuse. Otherwise, I didn't mean to come."

Judge's expression was one of absolute amazement.

"Here is some misunderstanding, evidently. Mrs. Richborough was kind enough to offer herself as chaperon to *you,* on learning that you were so anxious to see the house once more. . ."

The widow actually coloured, beneath her paint and powder. "Really, I'll never equivocate again as long as I live! Miss Loment seemed so unwilling to join us that there was positively nothing left to do except appeal to her sympathy. . . I feel an absolute criminal."

"Oh, it's *funny,* Mrs. Richborough!" said Isbel. "Don't start apologising or you'll spoil the joke."

"But surely, Miss Loment," said Judge, "you didn't for one minute imagine that I desired to fetch you all the way from Brighton merely to act as a companion to another lady? I must have made that clear in my letter."

"Oh, it's a mix-up, and that's all about it. Mrs. Richborough was obliging me, and I was under the impression that I was obliging her. When women start conferring favours on one another, there's no end to the complications. To show our thorough disinterestedness, we stick at nothing."

"It must certainly have been a most confusing situation for both of you," remarked Judge, smiling at last "However, the main point is we've got you here, by fair means or foul; and I don't think you need be in the least afraid of tittle-tattle, as we are both highly respectable people. If might suggest a compromise, you had better terminate your dispute of generosity by agreeing to chaperon each other, since in the eyes of the world I am such a dangerous person."

"Then what are we waiting for?" demanded Isbel cheerfully. "Lunch seems to be at an end."

They stayed for coffee, however, and then, while Judge went outside to prepare the car, Mrs. Richborough led the somewhat unwilling girl upstairs to her room, where for five unpleasant minutes she was forced to inhale an atmosphere almost nauseous with feminine perfume, while witnessing the elder woman's final applications of paint, powder, and salve. Refusing the use of these materials for herself, at the end of that time she broke away, and went downstairs alone.

She found Judge promenading before the hotel. A rather embarrassed discussion of the weather began.

"Thanks for the letter!" said Isbel, quietly and suddenly. "It *was* my hairpin."

"I decided as much; there's no one else it could have belonged to."

"Won't you tell me what was in that note you destroyed?"

"I can't—I can't. Say no more about it."

"Whose idea really was it, that I should come over today—yours or hers?"

"Mine, Miss Loment. She has nothing at all to do with the business. I am simply bringing her because you can't go with me alone."

"I'd rather it were anyone else. Who is she? Do you know anything about her?"

"Nothing, I fear, except that she's quite reputable. . . Don't you like her, then?"

"Not particularly—but we won't pay her the honour of talking about her. . . What are we to do today?"

"I thought we could make a desperate effort to get this mystery cleared up, once for all. . . I fear we must both recognise that things can't go on in the way they're doing. It's unfair to both of us."

Isbel gave him a half-frightened glance. "What's to prevent us from finishing *now*? Why need we take a still deeper plunge—for that's what it amounts to. . . or does it? What do you think—shall we really ever get any satisfaction? I'm fearfully uncertain. . ."

"You place a great responsibility on my shoulders, Miss Loment. . . To be quite truthful, I feel I have no right to ask you to proceed further.

I would not have written you as I did, except that I somehow had it firmly wedged in my head that the uncertainty was causing you great uneasiness. . ."

"It's half-killing me. . . We'll go. . . But what are we to do with that woman when we get there?"

"It hasn't occurred to me. It may be awkward, I can see."

"If we don't hurry up and plan something, we shall have her trailing after us all the time."

"Something may turn up, to give us our chance."

"That's most unlikely—nothing ever turns up when you want it to. We'd better contrive something after this style: while we are all three going over the house together, I'll accidentally become separated from you, and you must leave her while you hunt for me. We both know our respective stations."

"But if she insists on accompanying me. . . ?"

"Oh, she won't keep it up; she'll soon tire of tramping up and down stairs, and along interminable corridors, in her high-heeled boots—searching for a girl she's utterly callous about. Besides, she has a weak heart. . ."

"Did she say so?"

"No, but she has all the symptoms. . . Of course, you'll make a point of looking *upstairs* first."

Judge obviously was reluctant to assent to her plan. "I suppose we can think of nothing better. Apart altogether from putting a deliberate deceit on a defenceless and unsuspecting woman, we have to consider the circumstance that she will be alone in a large and gloomy house very likely upwards of half an hour; and you say her heart is not in good shape."

"I expect she'll survive the ordeal, and if it's any consolation to you, I fancy her own programme won't bear a great deal of looking at."

"What programme is that?"

"Oh, I don't pretend to know the details, Mr. Judge; only I'm pretty sure she's hatching something. Otherwise, why should she go to the trouble of *blackmailing* me into accompanying you today? I don't suppose you're aware of the fact that she openly threatened me with informing my aunt that I had met you privately at Worthing?"

"You didn't tell me that! . . . Upon my soul! . . . Solely for the purpose of getting you to come?"

"Yes. I refused at first. I wasn't very keen on her society, to tell you the truth."

"But what can her motive be for such conduct?"

"I have my ideas on the subject."

"I really must ask you. . ."

"I may be mistaken, but my belief is she wants to compromise me."

"But why?"

Isbel smiled cynically. "As a necessary preliminary to breaking off my intimacy with you, I imagine."

"You are telling me most astonishing things, Miss Loment. What interest is it of hers to break off this intimacy?"

"Oh, that's the simplest question of all to answer. To keep the matrimonial field clear for herself, of course. . . Didn't you know she had marked you down?"

"I cannot believe it," said Judge, halting to stare at her, in his bewilderment.

"If you don't know it, I expect everyone else does at your hotel." The words dropped from her lips with such dry assurance that he felt she must be possessed of special knowledge.

He was silent for a moment.

"This is a revelation indeed, Miss Loment! . . . I don't know what to say to it all. Now you speak of it, I confess I *have* had my suspicions once or twice lately, but I have always dismissed them as discreditable. . . But really, such a diabolical plot against the honour of a young girl is wholly unbelievable. It savours more of melodrama."

"Oh, I won't swear to that part of it, but there's something funny up, and I advise you to keep your eyes opened to the fullest possible extent. *I* mean to."

"I hardly feel like meeting her after this."

"You must, though—and you must go on behaving to her as nicely as ever. Remember, it's our only chance of going to the house together."

Mrs. Richborough herself at that moment appeared, descending from the hotel.

"I didn't tell you," said Isbel, "but we're returning to town next week."

"What! You're leaving Brighton? But this is very unexpected. Has your aunt changed her plans, or what?"

"I only knew last night. She thinks I am looking unwell."

"But you are not *feeling* unwell?"

"It's useless to deny that my nerves are a bit jangled," replied Isbel carelessly.

"Then she is giving up all idea of my house?"

"I can't say, Mr. Judge. I shall have a word in the matter. We shall see. Don't say anymore—here she comes."

The widow came up to them with a prepared smile. "I'm so frightfully sorry to have kept you both waiting. No doubt you've been saying hard things about me?"

"People evidently have spoilt you, Mrs. Richborough," returned Isbel. "When I turn my back on company, I invariably expect to be promptly forgotten."

"What ideal modesty! People always talk. The only problem is: have they been pitying us, or annihilating us? I'm not sure I wouldn't rather it were the second."

"Well, you're still alive," was the dry reply.

Judge opened the door of the car gravely, without committing himself to a word, and the ladies got in. While he was settling himself preliminary to starting, the widow turned to Isbel.

"I understood you might have something to say to each other, my dear; that's why I delayed."

"That was very kind of you."

"I do hope we're to be friends. I like you tremendously already."

"What for? I really can't see what I've done to make myself so beloved."

"Oh, it isn't what one does, but what one is. I think you have a perfectly wonderful character, for a girl."

Isbel did not even smile. "My dear Mrs. Richborough, If you were a man I should think you were trying to make love. As it is, I don't understand you in the least."

"Surely it is permissible for women to admire one another's natures? You are so sympathetic, and so tactful, my dear. I'm sure when we know each other better we shall get on splendidly together."

"What good qualities do *you* bring into the pool, Mrs. Richborough?"

"Alas, my dear! I have only one; and that is a *heart.*"

"So you are to do the feeling, while I am to do the sympathising; is that the arrangement?"

The widow gave a distant, rather melancholy smile.

"No one can deny that you are a very clever girl, and perhaps that is one more reason why I like you."

The dialogue was terminated by the abrupt starting of the car. Isbel glanced at her watch. It was half-past one.

XIV

IN THE SECOND CHAMBER AGAIN

At ten minutes to three, while they were all together in the library on the first floor, Mrs. Richborough and Judge were inspecting one of the corner shelves, with their backs turned upon her—thereby effectually excluding her from the conversation—Isbel seized the opportunity to slip quietly from the room. Descending on tip-toe the servants' staircase opposite, she found herself in the kitchens, through which she was obliged to pass in order to regain the hall. As she went by the foot of the main staircase, she heard her name being called. . . "Miss Loment! Miss Loment!" . . . It was Judge's voice. She had been missed already, and the mock search had commenced.

A short half-hour ago, when she had entered the hall from out of doors in company with the others, those strange stairs had not been there. Whether it was that her agitation prohibited the use of her reasoning faculties, or whether that her mind had become surfeited with marvels, it hardly occurred to her to doubt that she should see them now. Hurried to action by the distant hailing, she at once lifted her eyes, anxiously and fearfully, to the wall beyond the fireplace, while still hastening across the floor. . . *There they were!* . . .

She arrived at the foot of the staircase as in a dream, and stood a moment with one shoe poised on the bottom step, her gaze vainly directed towards the invisible top. Then, without changing a muscle of her face, she began to mount.

Halfway up, when the hall was already out of sight, her memory came back and she started piecing together the incidents of her last visit to that extraordinary region of the house. To allow herself time to thoroughly reconstruct everything, she seated herself sideways on one of the steps, staring fixedly downstairs, with twisted neck and eyes which saw nothing. . .

The more she recollected of that meeting with Judge, the greater became her disquietude; she kept starting nervously to rise, while the blood ebbed and flowed in her cheeks. If in that interview they had succeeded in keeping within the bounds of friendship, it was obviously it had only been by the exercise of great self-control; and, in view of his later confession, who could say what would now happen? The warm sympathy of their exchanges, their almost unseemly anxiety to lay aside all deception with each other, their mutual approval of one another's conduct—upon which the world would pass an altogether different judgement—and, lastly, her gift to him of that scarf, warm from her own neck: all this, as it grew slowly together in her mind, appeared to her as something which was irreconcilable with her true character, as something shameless and dreadful; it was like awaking by degrees to the awful temporary insanity. . . Only it was not insanity; it was not even an accidental expression of excited feelings, induced by the strange circumstances in which they had found themselves. It was worse than that. It sprang from the genuine and unfeigned emotion of both their hearts. . .

By what miraculous chance had they met there, at the same hour, on the same day, in the same unreal room of a house which, less than a month ago, she had not known the existence? Judge had not set foot in that weird room for eight years, while she had never been inside it before in her life—and now, suddenly, they meet there, and within a few minutes she has given him a tangible pledge of her favour. . .

It was more than chance; it was *fate*. Something—some strange influence in the house, was throwing them together. . . how far and for what purpose she dared not ask herself. It was of no use to disguise things. Every step they took—inside the house, or out of it—had the direct effect of entangling them more and more, and there could be but one end to it all; an end which bore a double face. The obverse face was noble, uplifting union with a man of unique character; the reverse face was social catastrophe. . .

She was a betrothed girl, and honour commanded she go back at once. It was untrue. . . she did not love Judge, she did love Marshall. On the last occasion she had met Judge by chance, therefore she was not at fault, but if now she persisted in repeating the adventure she would be committing a sin of conscience. And how would it be possible for her ever to hold up her head again among her friends, if she elected to act with such disgusting faithlessness towards a true-hearted man of her own age, in order to accept the sudden protestations of emotional affinity of an elderly widower? . . . She buried her face in her hands. . .

But it was out of the question to turn tail now, without first clearing things up. If she did, it would simply mean the whole torturing business over again—the same failure of memory, the same anxiety to find out what had happened, the same dallyings with Judge, the same surreptitious visits and counter-visits, the same humiliating scheming and deception, the same lowering of her entire moral and physical tone, and in the end. . . *exposure!* If she were so miserably weak and cowardly, so unsure of her own moral fibre, that she dared not meet a strange man in a private place for ten minutes, in order to finish with him once for all, then affairs had arrived at a very serious impasse, and she was deliberately turning her back on the only apparent means of escape from an impossible situation.

However much she dreaded it, there was really no alternative to her seeing Judge upstairs just this once more. . . not as stolen joy, but in order to put a definite end to their disagreeable intimacy. Exactly how this was to be effected she did not know, but, since he was a gentleman, he would of course make it his business to devise some plan. . . After all, this dreadful manor house was his, he was responsible for what went on inside it; if there were mysteries there requiring a solution, he had no earthly right to call upon *her* for assistance. . .

She got up and mechanically shook out her garments. Slowly climbing the remaining stairs, she again stood in the familiar ante-chamber, with its three doors. Without any hesitation whatever she advanced to the middle one, and, sharply turning the handle, let herself into the apartment, where last Monday she had met Judge.

Nothing was different. There were the same panelled walls, the same polished flooring, the same solitary couch at the end of the room. She cast a troubled glance round, and sat down, with heaving bosom, to wait. . .

Five minutes later the door was thrown open, and Judge walked in. He stopped where he was, looked anxiously at Isbel and at the same time pushed the door to, behind him, but failed to close it. Isbel gazed in his direction with equal earnestness, but she did not offer to rise.

"I've got away, as you can see," began Judge. "May I sit down?"

"Please!" She made space for him. They both sat in stiff attitudes, at some distance from each other.

There was an awkward pause, which Isbel broke by saying: "I don't wish to come here again, so we must think of some way of ending it."

"I quite understand."

"It's making my existence intolerable."

"It was madness on my part to accept that scarf. That's the root of all the mischief. I ought to have known that we should remember nothing of the circumstances under which it came into my possession."

"We were both to blame for that. It doesn't matter now. But I shan't come here again, so I wish to ask you to take steps to prevent a repetition."

"Very well. I'll write a note before we go down, and put it in my vest pocket, where I shall be sure to strike it. . . But are we not to see that other room?"

Isbel, glancing at him, uttered an involuntary little exclamation.

"What's the matter?" asked Judge.

"Nothing—but how extraordinarily young you look!"

"You are strangely altered, too. Not younger, not even more beautiful, I think, but. . . more *wonderful*. . . It's a weird, mystical room, there's no doubt."

"Have you still no idea where we are?"

"None."

She pointed towards the walls "All this is workmen's work."

"We daren't think otherwise. But the place is intensely dreamlike. . . and yet I can't remember having ever enjoyed a more poignant sense of actuality."

"Was it accident, or fate, that brought us here together last time? It has been puzzling me. It looks as if something—perhaps the house itself—were throwing us together, without our wills being in anyway consulted. . . Is such a thing possible, do you think?"

"We cannot think it of what possible advantage can it be to an unseen Power that I should be forced to play the part of a persecutor, and you that of a victim?"

"Aren't we both victims? To me we seem like moths fluttering round a lamp. I expect a moth has no memory, either—only instinct and a capacity for suffering. . . I see no end to it; we shall return here again and again, until our wings are burnt indeed!"

Her voice caught a little. Judge moved closer to her, and placed a hand on her sleeve, but lightly and without familiarity.

"We are not moths, but creatures endowed with reason, and we can blow our lamp out without waiting for the tragedy. If necessary, I will shut the place up, and go abroad for a time. It won't be long before you have forgotten all about the affair."

Isbel gave him a singular, half-wistful smile. "Have you sufficient strength of character to do this?"

"Yes; if I were once assured that your happiness is involved. To secure that, I would willingly burn the whole house to the ground."

"I know it."

"And I know that you know it; and that is my reward."

There was a break in the conversation, but she made no movement to disengage her arm. After a moment she said very quietly:

"It's just because you ask less than other men that I can afford to give you more. You understand that?"

"So let it be," replied Judge.

"Are you content?"

"I have confessed my feelings, and you have not withdrawn your friendship. That fixes our relations, and I have no desire to transgress the bounds laid down."

"Because your temper is naturally noble," said Isbel. "All the other men I have met have been plebeians, but you are made of different material, and that is why you act so differently. . . When I go downstairs again, I shall go downstairs indeed! . . ."

The were so absorbed in their talk that neither of them observed that the door had become pushed half-open, and that a figure stood on the threshold, watching them in silence.

It was Mrs. Richborough!

It did not appear how long she had been standing there, but suddenly Isbel looked up. She uttered a little scream, wrenched her arm free, and started to her feet. Judge followed the direction of her horrified stare, and swore under his breath; he also got up.

"I'm sorry if I've frightened you," said Mrs. Richborough quietly, without smiling. "I won't stay—but where are we, and what does it all mean?"

There was a tense silence.

"I'm afraid Miss Loment feels slightly upset at finding herself here," offered Judge at last, in a fairly firm voice. "I have been trying to reassure her. We met here by accident."

"But what part of the house is this? I thought the East Room was at the top, immediately under the roof?"

"So I believe."

"Then where are we?"

"Higher still, it appears. You know as much as I do about it, Mrs. Richborough. . . You followed me after all, then?"

"Yes. Your manner struck me as peculiar, and I was suspicious. I kept you in sight as far as the East Room, but there you shut the door after you, and I didn't venture to intrude at first. Your direction was so very decided that I felt positive it was a got-up thing. I listened outside for voices for some minutes, but, as everything was quite quiet, at last I did summon courage to enter. You weren't there, but I caught sight of another flight of stairs leading upwards, so very naturally I made use of them. And here I am."

Judge heard her to the end attentively, and then, turning half-away, began to whistle beneath his breath, between his teeth. Isbel, looking very distressed, sat down again.

"Has either of you ever been here before?" asked Mrs. Richborough, glancing first at one and then at the other.

"I have, a good many times, in former years," answered Judge.

"Then surely you have *some* idea where we are?"

"I haven't." His tone was dry and decided.

Mrs. Richborough launched a queer look at him, and began to gaze around her restlessly.

"What's in that other room?"

"Which one?"

"On the right, as you come up the stairs. The other one can't be anything much."

"What makes you say that?" questioned Isbel, surprised out of her silence.

"Intuition. . . But what *is* in that right-hand room*?*"

"I've never been inside it," replied Judge.

"Why ever not? Most likely it's the key to the whole place. *Someone* ought to go in. May I go?"

"I don't care to ask you, Mrs. Richborough. It's totally unexplored, and you might quite conceivably meet with an unpleasant experience."

"I don't view these things from the common standpoint. For me, there's nothing whatever terrifying in the supernatural. . . Have I your permission to go?"

"Of course—but perhaps we ought to accompany you?"

"Oh, no—there's not the slightest necessity. Besides, you have your talk to finish. I'm perfectly conscious of having interrupted you."

Isbel clutched the couch on either side of her with her hands, and looked up. "Have you nothing to say about. . . your surprise. . . at finding us together like this?"

Mrs. Richborough gave a strange, but not unpleasant smile.

"No, I have nothing to say about that."

"But, of course, you. . . put the worst construction. . ."

"No. . ." She passed her hand across her eyes. "A change of some sort has come over me. It is this terribly unreal place, I think. Your meeting is not what I expected to find. You must be struggling *against* your hearts, both of you. . . No, I have nothing to say."

"And yet you came to look for us?"

"Yes, I did; but it is all different. As I came upstairs I *hated* you both, and vowed revenge—I confess it. But now I can't even remember how I came to be like that. All that state of mind suddenly seems so trivial and unimportant."

She was about to move towards the door.

"Mrs. Richborough! . . ." said Isbel abruptly.

"What is it?"

"Why were you so anxious to bring me here today?"

"You must know that without my telling you. Here all things are so transparent to all of us."

"You meant to tell Mr. Stokes, didn't you?"

The older woman looked down at her calmly. "Yes, I meant to restore you to your duty. But now I no longer pretend to know where your duty lies. Let me go now, my dear. All that is ancient history; everything has changed."

Isbel said nothing more, but allowed her to leave the room. The door closed behind her.

Judge resumed his seat.

"We need not fear this development," he said slowly. "She will remember nothing."

"So much the worse, for she will go back to her plots and schemes. You haven't thought of that?"

The suggestion startled him. "You think so?"

"How can it be otherwise? Oh, if her present mood lasted, I should never, never wish to speak ill of her. But we know it will disappear with her memory. What is to be done?"

He preserved silence for a few moments.

"After all, there is no cause for alarm. She will demand her price, and we shall pay it."

"No, no; she will accept nothing short of the whole—I know her. In that she will be disappointed, and so she will do whatever mischief she can. Oh, I'm quite sure of it."

"What do you mean by 'the whole'?"

"She intends to marry you."

"And failing that? . . ."

"Failing that, she will dishonour me—or perhaps she means to dishonour me in any case. You heard with your ears what she said."

"But if I consented to marry her I should, of course, make her silence a condition." The words came in a very low voice, as he bent his head towards the floor.

"What do you mean?" she demanded, sharply. "How could you marry her? You don't love her."

"No."

"Then it would be *wicked* of you! . . . What put that awful thought in your head? I can't understand."

"Yet it would solve other difficulties, too."

"What difficulties? What difficulties *can* a wrong marriage solve? It would be criminal."

"Some such decisive step must be taken to end the situation. Our friendship won't continue to pass unnoticed."

"You wish to terminate it, then?"

"For your sake; not mine."

"And to achieve that result you accept a living death? . . . But perhaps you do really love her?"

"No."

Isbel laid her hand on his arm. "Promise me never to think of this again. It is absolute madness. We will find someother way out of our troubles. Promise me."

"You may be sure of one thing," replied Judge, looking at her steadily; "I shall not renounce my moral right to devote my life to your service, except as the very last resource. Beyond that I cannot go."

Suddenly Isbel raised her head and seemed to listen to some sound outside the room.

"What was that?" she asked quickly.

"It sounded extremely like a stiff window-shutter being jerked open; it's probably Mrs. Richborough in the next room."

He had scarcely spoken when another noise, more distinct and far more peculiar, struck their ears.

"It's music!" said Isbel, shaking from head to foot, and attempting unsuccessfully to rise.

"Yes. . . A bass viol—but some way off. I can't conceive what it can be. Would you wait here while I go and investigate?"

"No, you mustn't—I won't have it! I won't be left. . ."

Judge sat down again, and they went on listening in silence. The low, rich, heavy scraping sound certainly did resemble that of a deep-toned stringed instrument, heard from a distance, but to Isbel's imagination, it resembled something else as well. She thought she recognised it as the must of that dark upstairs corridor, which she had heard on her first visit to the house. But this time it was ever so much nearer, fuller, and more defined; the electric buzzing had resolved itself into perfectly distinct vibrations. . . A tune was being played, so there was no doubt about the nature of the noise. It was a simple, early-English rustic air—sweet, passionate and haunting. The sonorous and melancholy character of the instrument added a wild, long-drawn-out charm to it which was altogether beyond the range of the understanding and seemed to belong to other days, when feelings were more poignant and delicate, less showy, splendid, and odourless. . . After the theme had been repeated once, from beginning to end, the performance ceased, and was succeeded by absolute stillness.

They looked at each other.

"How beautiful! . . . but how perfectly awful!" said Isbel.

"Do you wish to go downstairs at once?"

Some seconds passed before she answered.

"No, I'll stay. How could we leave it without finding out? . . . We'll go in there in a minute. I don't wish to while *she's* there. Let's finish what we were saying. . . You mustn't commit that crime."

"Your honour comes before everything."

"You don't belong to her." She drew a long breath before proceeding. . . "You belong to me."

"I do not belong to you."

"Yes—you know it is so."

"I beg you to reflect upon what you're saying. You are not yourself at present. Don't use language you will be sure to regret afterwards."

Isbel ignored his interruption.

"I have lied too much to my own heart, and it's time I were honest. They talk of faith and loyalty, but how can one be loyal to others if one is not first loyal to one's own nature? There cannot be a greater sin than to pretend that our feelings are what in reality they are not."

"This is no place for such deliberations. I beg you earnestly to say no more here and now. Reserve it until later."

"No, I must speak. If I don't speak out now, when shall I get another chance? . . . My engagement has been a ghastly mistake. . . It must have always been in the back of my mind, but now I see it all clearly for the first time. . ." She crouched nearly double, and covered her face with her two hands.

Judge, much agitated, got up.

"I can't listen to this. It's impossible for me to discuss such a subject. It rests entirely between you and your own heart."

"I made the terrible blunder of imagining that identity of tastes and friends means love. I took things too much for granted. . . His nature had no depth. . . He has never *suffered*. It isn't in him."

"You must think it over in quietness. Say no more now."

She sat up suddenly, and stared at him.

"You throw me to him, then?—you who profess to have such ideal love for me!"

Judge was silent.

"So you don't love me?"

"In the end you will understand that I love you deeply and truly."

She slowly rose to her feet. "Then what do you advise me to do?"

"Do nothing at all, but wait."

"You have no questions for *me?*"

"What questions?"

"I love no one but you," said Isbel. She caught his hand, and crushed it hard in hers; then abruptly turned her back on him. . . Judge stood like one transfixed.

At the same moment Mrs. Richborough came into the room. Her natural pallor was intensified, while her face was set and drawn, as though she had received a shock.

"Oh, what's the matter?" exclaimed Isbel, taking a step in her direction.

The older woman swayed, as if about to fall. Judge hastened forward to support her.

"I'm afraid I've just seen a sight which I can only regard as a *warning*. As you look out of the window there is a man, with his back turned. He looked round, and then I saw his face. I can't describe it. . . I think I'll go downstairs, if you don't mind."

The others looked at one another.

"Shall I take you down?" asked Judge.

"If you would assist me to the head of the stairs, I shall be all right."

He asked no questions, but at once supported her from the room. Isbel followed. On arriving at the top of the staircase, he lent the dazed woman his arm down the first few steps, then watched her out of sight before rejoining his companion.

Again they gazed at each other.

"You heard what she said," remarked Judge quietly. "Under the circumstances I don't feel justified in asking you to accompany me into that room."

"Are you going?"

"Yes, I'm going."

"Then I shall go, too."

XV

THE MUSIC OF SPRING

They walked over to the right-hand door, which Judge, after turning the handle, at once kicked wide open with his foot. . . A sudden and unanticipated flood of brilliant sunshine, streaming through the room form an open window on the further side, momentarily blinded them, so that they staggered back with the shock.

Judge was the first to recover himself.

"It's all right, we can go in. The room's empty."

Isbel hastened to the window. It was breast-high. There was no glass in it, but it possessed a stout wooden shutter, opening outwards, which at present was swung to its full extent squarely against the outside wall. The aperture of the window was so narrow that there was barely space for their two heads together, and she found her smooth cheek grazing his harsh one.

From out of doors came not only the sunlight but the song of birds, the loud sighing of the wind in its passage through the trees, and an indescribable fresh, sweet smell, as of meadow grass, turned-up earth, and dew-drenched flowers. It seemed more like spring than autumn.

"Where are we, then?" was Isbel's first inquiry, uttered in a tone of bewilderment. "How do we come to be to high up from the ground?"

"I don't recognise any of it. It's all new to me."

From the foot of the house wall, forty feet below, the free country started. Judge stared in vain for familiar landmarks—the more he gazed, the more puzzled he became. Not only had his own grounds disappeared, but neither in the foreground nor in the distance was there a single sign of human occupancy or labour. Look where he would, fields, hedgerows, roads, lanes, houses, had vanished entirely out of the landscape.

A bare hillside of grass and chalk, perhaps a couple of hundred feet high, fell away sharply from the house, to terminate in a miniature valley along which a brook, glittering in the sunlight, wound its way. Beyond it there was a corresponding hill up, but not so steep or high; and here the woods began; an undulating but unbroken forest appeared to extend right to the horizon, many miles distant. The intensely blue sky was adorned with cirrus-clouds, while the dazzling sun was high above their heads, about half a point to the right. Apart, altogether, from the strangeness of the scenery, anything less like a late October afternoon would be hard to imagine; the forests were brilliantly green, many of the smaller, isolated trees in the valley were crowned with white blossom, while the air itself held that indefinable spirit of wild sweetness which is inseparable from a spring morning.

"Just look at that man!" said Isbel, suddenly.

He was sitting on the slope of the hill, directly opposite their window and not a stone's throw from them, but half hidden by the crest of the small hollow which he had selected for his perch, which explained why they had not previously noticed him. He sat motionless, facing the valley, with his back to the house; what he was doing there they could not imagine. It was his extraordinary attire which had evoked Isbel's exclamation. Only his head, the upper half of his back, and one out-stretched leg were visible; but the leg was encased in a sage-green trouser, tightly cross-gartered with yellow straps, the garment on his back resembled, as far as could be seen, a purple smock, and the hair of his hatless head fell in a thick, bright yellow mane as far as his shoulders.

Notwithstanding Isbel's amazement, she began to laugh.

"No wonder poor Mrs. Richborough was startled! Is it a man, or a tulip?"

"He looks like an ancient Saxon come to life," replied Judge, also laughing, but more moderately.

"Ulf, perhaps."

"Very likely," he agreed, without understanding her.

"Cry out and *ask* him if his name's Ulf."

"But who was Ulf?"

"Don't you know? Why he's the man who built your house. The trolls ran away with him, poor fellow! and probably he's been sitting here ever since, yearning to get back home again. . . Do call out."

"You really want me to call?"

"If you don't I shall, and that will be immodest."

Judge shouted at the top of his voice. The man neither responded nor turned his head.

"Again!" commanded Isbel, laughing. "Louder—much louder! As if someone were running off with property of yours. . ."

This time Judge roared, and then Isbel added her strange clanging cry twice or thrice, laughing between whiles; but still they were unable to attract his attention.

Temporarily abandoning the effort, she turned her head and glanced sideways at Judge, with an almost joyous expression. "We can't be in October. That hawthorn's blooming. . . and look at those beeches over there, with their pale-green, transparent leaves. . . Hark! . . ."

They kept quiet for a minute. . . A distant cuckoo was calling. The cry was regularly repeated, at very short intervals.

Judge rubbed his eyes, in actual doubt whether he were awake or dreaming. "It's spring, sure enough—but how can it be?"

"Oh, if we could only get down into it all!"

Both instinctively measured the wall beneath them with their eyes, but the distance to the ground was too great, the footholds were too precarious.

She leant further out, inhaling the sweet, fragrant air in deep breaths, and sighing it out again. . . "Beautiful!—beautiful! . . ."

Then once more she became fascinated by the man.

"It can't be true. Such men don't exist—at least, nowadays. It's an optical illusion. If it were a real person he would answer us."

Judge hailed him again, but without result. A moment later, however, the man stooped to pick something up, and when he regained his sitting posture they caught a glimpse of a fiddle-shaped instrument in his hand, somewhat larger than a modern viola. Wasting no time in preliminaries, he swung his bow across it, and at once started to repeat the air they had heard already from the other room.

Isbel, drawing back a little, rested her elbow on the window-sill and her face on her elbow, in order better to concentrate her thoughts on the music. Judge retired altogether into the room, to make space for her. The tone of the instrument, notwithstanding its small size, was midway in depth between that of a violoncello and that of a contra-bass, and the low, slow scrape of its strings had a peculiarly disturbing effect upon her feelings. The theme had a strange, archaic flavour, as though it had come down through the centuries, yet it was so appropriate that Isbel could almost fancy it to be the voice of the landscape. It was hauntingly beautiful, and full of queer surprises; each long, sonorous note contained a world of music in itself, but it was the powerful, yet delicate and passionate *thought* slowly being developed as the air proceeded which stirred her so exceedingly.

While she stood listening, feelings which she had not had for ten years suddenly returned to her, and she realised, as in a flash, how far down the hill of life she had already travelled. That complex state of youth, composed of wildness, melancholy, audacity, inspiration, and hope, was momentarily restored to her, but only as a memory, as if for the purpose of mocking her. . . As the music finished, tears stood in her eyes, and her heart was choking, yet she was not unhappy. . .

Judge approached her from behind. . . "Isbel!" . . .

"It was like the voice of spring," she said, without turning round. "You are tortured, but you don't know what is happening to you."

"Music must have been like that at one time."

"Did you feel it, too?"

"It must be very, very old." . . . They hardly knew what they were saying to each other.

The musician had sunk back into a reclining position, so that only the crown of his head was visible. Isbel at last looked round. She caught sight of Judge's face, with its contracted muscles and pained expression, but instantly left that to glance at an envelope which he held in his hand.

"What have you there?"

He handed it to her. "I found it lying on the floor."

The envelope was addressed to Mrs. Richborough, at the Metropole, but its contents had been abstracted. On the back had been scribbled very roughly in ink the first few bars of the tune they had just heard.

"It has probably got blown down," suggested Judge. "She must have left it for the ink to dry, and forgotten it, in her alarm."

Isbel looked at it for some moments, and then slipped it in her hand-bag. "That woman will take notes on the Day of Judgement. But why shouldn't she? That music could have meant nothing to her."

"What does it mean to us?"

They stood close by the window, but not looking out. Isbel's face bore a singular smile.

"It means something, I think."

"What?"

"Do you feel nothing?"

"I feel great happiness, which I am striving not to account for."

"It means what spring means," said Isbel.

She suddenly threw both arms around his neck, clutching him tightly, but at the same time turning away in such a manner that it was the back of her hair only which brushed his cheek. . . When she disengaged herself violently a few seconds later, her face was hot, and she was in tears. . .

Judge breathed hard, and looked dark under the eyes, but he made no attempt to draw nearer.

"What's wrong, Isbel?"

"You are cruel! . . ."

"I cruel. . . ?"

"Oh, go away from me—altogether! . . ."

She turned her back on him, and bent her head.

"Will you listen to me? . . . I have no right. . ."

"I know. You've told me a thousand times already. . . You put law first, love second."

"I demand a very small assurance from you, but that assurance I must have. Are you free now?"

"I won't say—I refuse to answer. I'll have everything, or nothing from you." She wheeled round furiously. "If I'm not worth that, I'm worth nothing at all. . ."

The scent of violets and primroses seemed to come in with the breeze through the open window, while Isbel's voice, like soft brass, thrilled the ear with its strange range of tones. She stood there, confronting him—a warm, passionate girl, in sweet clothes—as though she were a second self, his own soul reflected from a magic mirror. Among the whole world of human beings, they two alone possessed the entry into each other's innermost nature. . . That delicately-modelled woman's mouth, which had just uttered such words of scorn—if he pleased, in another instant it should break into the loveliest smiles. . .

As they faced one another in silence, the music out-of-doors recommenced without warning. It was the same everlasting tune. Isbel twitched impatiently, and abruptly turned her back on Judge again. . . But though the theme was the same, the execution was markedly different that she had to listen, despite her agitation. The playing was faster, higher, lighter, and *staccato*. The lingering, haunting sweetness was transformed into a delicate and triumphant dance; the very sunshine which flooded the room seemed suddenly to become more joyous and ethereal. . . Without understanding, or wishing to understand, how the change had been effected, she felt her brow clearing, her heart lightening. . .

Judge waited until the last note had died down, and then said, in a low voice:

"I find I'm not as strong as I thought I was. . . so I'm yours, to do what you like with. Tell me to jump out of the window, and I'll do it. You're the only person in the world for me."

DAVID LINDSAY

XVI

THE MUSICIAN DEPARTS

Isbel commenced unbuttoning her left-hand glove, with slightly trembling fingers.

"Something is to go out our the window, but not you," She removed the diamond ring from her third finger, and eyed it pensively, before handing it to him. . . "Throw it out! Let strange find strange. I never should have worn it."

"Better to return it to the giver."

"As long as I carry it about with me, I haven't cast off the past. Do as I say. That episode is finished."

Judge, without further demur, took the ring to the window and dropped it out.

"That's done!" said Isbel, drawing a deep breath. "We shall have no more anxiety from that quarter."

Raising her ungloved hand, he bent over and kissed it submissively. She offered no resistance, but closed her eyes, as if to think the better, reopening them only when he had relinquished her fingers.

"Had your wife been still alive, would you have done as much for my sake, I wonder?"

"Don't doubt it. I would have sacrificed everything. But let the poor girl rest in peace. Fortunately, my loyalty wasn't put to the test during her lifetime."

"That magic word 'loyalty'! How can we be loyal to those to whom we don't naturally belong? You mean, fortunately you were enabled to act a living lie with her, without either of you suspecting the fact. . . You *know* you never loved her."

"What has been, has been. Whatever we felt towards each other, after all, she was my dear companion. You can't grudge her that."

Isbel laughed lightly. "I grudge her nothing. If you assured me you *loved* her, even I should accept your word. . . But you didn't. Love doesn't come twice in a lifetime. . . However, to avoid competition, it seems I must aim at higher things than being a mere dear companion."

"You must be aware that, in that sense, companionship is impossible between us," said Judge, in a low voice.

"Tell me why?"

"Because I am a man, and you are a beautiful girl, and all our ways and thoughts are strange and foreign to each other. Because my place is not standing face to face with you, exchanging incomprehensible ideas, but at your feet, smothering the hem of your skirt with kisses. . ." He stopped abruptly.

Her eyes danced. "But why waste precious kisses on inanimate cloth?"

"You're quite justified in laughing—I know my language sounds exaggerated. . . Pardon me, I'm excited!"

"And I—am I cool, do you think? . . . Now finish it all—and kiss me quickly! . . ."

Judge looked at her slowly. "You grant me this favour without my asking it?"

"Do you want it in writing, to make quite sure? . . . Oh, what are we here for? Why have we been brought to this place, except for this very one purpose? For half an hour I've done nothing else but count the minutes disappearing, one by one. . ."

"Isbel!" He approached her, almost as if disbelieving.

"Did you imagine that women's feelings had been left out of my anatomy?" laughed Isbel, pressing both cheeks with her fingers in an automatic attempt to cool them.

But as they were on the point of meeting, the music sounded again through the open window. Its scrape was so strangely insistent that they remained where they were until the interruption should come to an end; a moment afterwards, however, Isbel walked quietly to the window to see what could be seen, resuming her former attitude of leaning one arm on the sill.

The tune was as before, but once more its interpretation was varied. The gaiety had gone out of it, and it now possessed a swift, smooth strength which curiously suggested an incoming tide. Neither of the other versions had been half as beautiful; it was like a quick, tragic, irresistible summary of all which had gone before. Nothing had changed in the landscape. The sun shone, the trees waved, the brook glittered at the foot of the chalk hill, the musician remained half-concealed, half-visible, as his body swayed in unison with the rhythm of the theme. The entering breeze brought with it the smell of growing life, while, as an undertone to the music, many a soft cry of nature reached Isbel's ear. But as she continued to listen it seemed to her as if the world were at last moving, after a long, enchanted dream—as if a current had begun to run, and things could no longer be what they had been hitherto. . .

Her heart deepened. She felt suddenly that she had up to now been playing with life, but that reality had at length clutched her in its grasp, and now she must show what stuff she was made of. She was like a bather for whom a river proves too strong, and who is being walked downstream step by step, struggling in vain for footholds, until her waist is covered, and she must either swim or resign herself to be carried away to death. . . Her old happiness was past recovery. It rested with herself whether she were to be borne along backwards, looking after it despairingly, or whether she should throw herself audaciously into this new element, confiding in her strength and courage to bring her to safety. . . She realised that this was the moment she had been waiting for all her life. . .

The music stopped. Isbel faced round towards Judge, but did not stir from the window.

"These interruptions have a strangely agitating effect," he said, with a quiet smile. "Apparently he means neither to take notice of us nor leave us in peace. I see you are rather deeply moved."

"And you are not?"

"When *you* are present, music can be no more than a decoration of life. You are the centre of the piece, and the disturbing factor. If he plays again, I shall suggest that we return to the other room. We have seen everything here there is to see."

"You wish to resume where we left off, but I don't think we can. . . Henry, can't you understand that all this has a meaning? Don't you see that it's carrying us higher and higher? If you have forgotten your own words, I haven't."

"What words?"

"We were talking of tests. You said that one test of love is the craving to sacrifice oneself. At the time, I didn't understand you, but it was fearfully true. When a woman loves a man, there are no half-measures with her—she wishes to give him everything. Of course, 'sacrifice' isn't the right word to express it. A gift like that gives nothing up. . ."

Judge trembled slightly, in spite of his control. "Why do you say all this? I want neither sacrifices nor gifts from you, and you know it."

"But if I offer it?"

There was a short silence.

"Let me understand you," said Judge, "for perhaps we are at cross purposes. What is it you are offering me?"

"*Myself*," was the low-spoken reply.

Overcome by her own daring, without waiting for his response, she turned her back on him again, and stared out of the window.

With a dull shock, she perceived that the musician had risen at last to his full height. His tall, broad, gaily-attired figure was visible from top to toe, but his face was still turned away. He held his instrument by the neck with one hand, and seemed to be contemplating a descent to the foot of the hill. Isbel immediately glanced round to Judge.

"Henry, he's up now."

He joined her at the window.

"I thought he was going to sit there forever," said Isbel. "He seemed a part of the landscape. Will he turn round now, do you think?"

"It's an extraordinary business," muttered Judge. "He's real enough, but what man goes about in that sort of costume?"

"Or plays that sort of music? . . . I've a feeling that if he's going we'd better make haste. After he's gone, things will be different. I don't know whether we ought to attract his attention, or not."

Judge continued staring at the man in silence. Although the sun shone and the sky remained clear, with but few clouds, the tree-tops were sighing and swaying in greater agitation than before, and little, swirling wind-flurries kept coming and going in the air, freshening the room, and swinging the outside shutter to and fro with a harsh, musical creak.

"Is there no way of getting down?" demanded Isbel, the next minute. "It's awful to be shut up here in this box of a room while all that's going on. . . If we walked on and on through those woods, where should we come to?"

He sighed. "You're right. Our place is down there, in God's fresh air. . . But it's most remarkable he doesn't once look round. Can it be that he's sublimely unconscious of the existence of a house behind him?"

"No, he knows well enough. . . But I mean to see his face—if not now, another time. . . Look! he's off. . ."

The musician had begun to walk down the steep hillside with short steps, digging his heels into the turf for security. They watched him, fascinated, until he reached the bottom, when, instead of proceeding straight ahead up the opposite hill, he moved to the left along the bank of the stream. Though his action was quite leisurely, he never once paused or turned his head, so doubtless he was making for a destination. In a few minutes he would be out of sight, round the bend of the valley.

"It's too late now, but why didn't you call out to him again?" demanded Isbel. "I purposely refrained from asking you to, as I wanted to see what you would do."

"You attach such importance to it?"

"He brought us together. It was his music I heard the first time I came to Runhill, and it's plain to see he's had a hand in everything. It's natural one should want to see one's benefactor."

Judge led the way into the room, and once more they faced each other; she cast her eyes down, her arms falling limply on either side.

"I was frightened on your account, Isbel."

"But that is not what I want."

"What do you want?"

"I want you to feel what I feel. I want you to feel that as long as you are with me nothing can hurt either of us. Fear spells cold blood. But I think you can't be passionate. . . or else you wouldn't scorn my gift so."

"You think I do?"

"I *know* you do, for otherwise you would have accepted it."

"I have accepted it, and you're blind and foolish not to have seen it at once."

Isbel's eyes leapt to his face with a flash. "You accept my full love?"

"Yes, your full love," said Judge, setting his jaw hard. "There's no other kind worth the price we're paying. Be it so! . . . Bit I accept it in deep humility, for the gift is far too rich, and I have done nothing to deserve it. . . I shall dedicate the rest of my life to your service."

She approached him unsteadily.

"You must know that such a gift can't be paid for by service. There can only be one return for passion, and that's passion. If you haven't that to give, I want nothing."

"That you shall have in full measure," replied Judge.

He moved forward to embrace her.

At the same moment, quite suddenly, the sun went in, the wind ceased, and every outside sound stopped, as if cut off by a screen. The brightness of the room changed to twilight, while the air became perceptibly colder, and, at the same time stale-smelling. Judge's upraised arm fell slowly to his side, as he mechanically shrank back. Both turned their heads inquiringly towards the window. Then Isbel walked over to it, almost with reluctance, to look out.

"Henry, come here quickly! . . ."

He was already beside her. The landscape they were looking at was no longer the same. Immediately beneath them were the familiar grounds of Runhill Court; the chalk hill, diminished in height, had become the sloping lawn, with its continuation of the field they had traversed on the day of the picnic; in the background were other fields innumerable, with roads, lanes, and cottages. The unbroken forest of fresh green trees was transformed into scattered tracts of woodland, the prevailing colour of whose leaves was russet. The sun had disappeared; the country was wrapped in a misty dusk. The musician was nowhere to be discovered.

They gazed at each other in consternation, during which time their excitement rapidly subsided.

"Are we dreaming now, or were we dreaming before?" asked Isbel earnestly, laying her hand on his arm.

"We can't doubt this, at all events."

"Wasn't that real, then? Have we been the fools of our senses?"

"I fear it looks extremely like it."

"What, has it *all* been false?"

Judge shook his head grimly, but did not answer at once. . . "Anyway, it has happened in time. There's no harm done but what we can cover up and forget. We must be thankful for small mercies."

She turned fiery-red. "Has it really come to that?"

"At least, as you, too, have been involved, you will acquit me of deliberate wrong-doing. I fear it's hopeless trying to reconstruct our state of mind, or to understand what has taken place. Some unpleasant agency has been at work."

They went back into the room.

"So you don't love me?" demanded Isbel quietly.

"Yes, I love you."

"You know that, if our senses are restored, my ring is not restored?"

"Unfortunately, I know it only too well."

"So it means that your old generosity has come back?"

They stood for a long time, looking away from each other. Then, with death in her heart, Isbel started to put on her glove.

"We had better go downstairs again."

He bowed with stern gravity, and at once moved to the door, which he held open to allow her to pass out. She walked straight across to the stairs, without once turning her head to see if he were following.

The hall, when she reached it, was in dusk. Her watch told her it that it was nearing five o'clock. She looked dully around her, remembering nothing of what had occurred to her during the past hour and a half, but somehow, confusedly wondering why Judge had failed to descend that staircase with her—though, as a matter of fact, she did not even know whether he had been up there.

XVII

In the Twilight

The staircase had vanished, the house was in silence, evening was closing in, and her companions were absent. Isbel's heart throbbed heavily, she felt sick and weak, yet she thought she ought to go upstairs to look for them. She knew that Judge would not have departed without her. She considered that it would be best if she were to go straight upstairs to the East Room.

The prospect of visiting that remote part of the house so late in the day did not inspire her with any enthusiasm, but anything was preferable to waiting about in that awful hall. It was most singular why they should be so long. She made her way upstairs slowly, stopping at every sixth step to listen for sounds; but all was quiet as a tomb. As she groped her passage along the nightlike corridor at the top of the house, it occurred to her for the first time that she had never yet seen the East Room, though all her acquaintances seemed to have done so. She smiled rather contemptuously. Well, it would complete her experience of the place!

The door stood wide open. It was dim twilight within, and the apartment did not strike her as very noteworthy. It was small and square, with a single window on the far side; very poorly furnished. But as she stood at the door, looking in, her eyes immediately fell upon something which completely took away all her interest in the room itself. Mrs. Richborough was lying extended on the floor, with Judge kneeling beside her!

She rushed forward quickly. "Whatever's the matter, Mr. Judge? Is she ill?"

He looked up from bathing her forehead and lips with the contents of a pocket-flask.

"It's a swoon, and rather a bad one. I couldn't leave her, to come down to you."

"How did it happen?"

"I don't know. She was lying like this when I came down."

Isbel turned hastily from the unconscious woman to look at Judge. "Then you have been *up?*"

"Yes. And you?"

"Yes; but I remember nothing—nor, of course, you, either?"

"Nothing." He went on dabbing Mrs. Richborough's forehead.

"Is that doing her any good? Hadn't we better try and get her downstairs?"

"Her pulse is stronger, and I think she is coming round. It's hopeless to think of a doctor in these parts. If we can get her in the car, we'll soon run her down to Worthing. She must have had a fright of some sort."

"But how came she to find her way up here?"

"I suppose she looked everywhere for me. . . I've been staring at something on the floor over there for some while, but haven't been able to get up to investigate. It looks like a ring, or a brooch. She may have dropped it in falling."

Isbel, following the direction of his finger, detected the article, and picked it up. It proved to be a lady's diamond ring.

"It *is* a ring—and a rather nice one. It's very much like mine."

As she spoke the words, she instinctively felt for her engagement ring beneath her glove. . . It was not there! . . . She whipped off the glove, in dismay. Her third finger was ringless.

The recovered ring fitted it perfectly.

"It *is* mine!" she went on, with a desperate effort to keep calm, but unable to keep a slight break out of her voice.

"What! You surely must be mistaken."

"It's my engagement ring and ought to have been on my finger."

They stared at each other.

"You are sure?"

"Yes, I am quite sure."

"Then what is it doing here, Miss Loment? I can't understand it. You haven't been in this room before?"

"I have never been in this room before in my life. And I wore this ring at lunch today."

She retained it on her finger and replaced her glove over it. At the same time, Mrs. Richborough's face and neck stirred uneasily, and her eyelids flickered. Judge remained on his knees.

"How are we to understand it, do you suppose?" demanded Isbel, after a long pause, in the increasing darkness.

"I will not suggest what I don't think, Miss Loment, and I may not suggest what I do think."

"Oh, I know what you mean—and it's *ghastly!* It can't be. . ." Her face suddenly crimsoned; she felt as if she were on fire. "But perhaps I don't know what you mean. What *do* you mean?"

"I cannot say. But I can give you a piece of counsel. You came here today to end a mystery, and you have started a still worse one. Things can't go on like this; so I strongly advise that you make this your last visit to my house. This is the second time something has happened without your knowledge or consent."

"It's the uncertainty which is so horrible. . . Oh, can't *something* be done? Have you no initiative at all, Mr. Judge? You call yourself a man."

"It is high time to retrace our steps. We have already gone too far. I think my best plan will be to shut the house up altogether. I think I will do that."

He applied himself to moistening Mrs. Richborough's lips with the brandy. Her limbs began to move restlessly; it was evident that she was on the verge of regaining consciousness. After a moment or two he again looked up.

"I have only to express my sincere repentance at having invited you here this afternoon, Miss Loment. Of course, I should not have done so, and I am very sorry for it. My only excuse is that I knew no more than yourself."

She made no reply.

Mrs. Richborough at last opened her eyes. Judge, bending lower, obliged her to take a sip of the brandy, and the powerful stimulant had a nearly instant effect upon her heart. She struggled into a sitting posture, supported by his arm, and smiled wanly.

"Where am I? What has happened?"

"It's I—Mr. Judge—and this is Miss Loment. You have fainted."

"How idiotic!"

He forced her to swallow another mouthful of the spirit, and the colour started to return to her cheeks.

"You'll be all right in a minute or two. We'll get you downstairs to the car, make you comfortable, and run you home in less than no time. Feeling better already, aren't you?"

"But so absurdly shaky! . . . . I remember now. I had a sudden fright. It was horrid, and I was all alone."

"We'll hear about it later; never mind now."

With Isbel's assistance he succeeded in raising her to her feet. She was established in the chair, while the girl set her attire to rights. She started looking round on the floor uneasily.

"There should be a ring on the ground somewhere. Can you see it?"

"It has been picked up," said Isbel shortly.

"Oh!"

"It belongs to me. Can you tell me how it comes to be in this room, Mrs. Richborough?"

"It fell down from the wall. I did not know it was yours."

Judge and Isbel exchanged glances.

"How do you mean 'it fell down from the wall'?"

"It does sound stupid, but so it happened. That's what frightened me. It seemed to tumble on to the middle of the floor, from nowhere at all."

"But you said from the wall. Which wall?"

Mrs. Richborough turned weakly in her chair, and pointed behind her. "That wall. Where the stairs were previously. It rolled on to the floor, and I was just going to pick it up when I must have fainted."

"But what stairs are you alluding to?" asked Judge.

She smiled, closed her eyes, and was silent for a moment.

"How can I explain? It sounds incredible, but I saw a flight of stairs in the middle of that wall, ascending out of sight. I actually went up them—or could I have dreamt it all? I'm afraid my mind is all upside-down this afternoon."

Isbel coughed dryly, and glanced at her watch. Judge again pressed his flask on the widow.

"I won't, thanks. My heart is scarcely in a state to stand over-stimulation. If you could help me, I think I could make my way downstairs. That would be best for everybody."

Judge offered her his arm. On getting outside, he shut and locked the door of the room, putting the key in his pocket.

"You had better lead the way, Miss Loment. Take my torch."

Slowly and with frequent pauses, they passed through the corridor and descended the stairs to the hall. Judge was about to proceed outside, but Mrs. Richborough asked to be allowed to sit down, to recover her strength.

"Tell me," she said, after a minute, "where did you both get to? I can't understand what happened."

"Perhaps we have been where you have been, Mrs. Richborough," replied Isbel coldly.

"Oh! . . . Do you mean that? Are you pretending you saw those extraordinary stairs, too?"

"Unless they were a figment of your brain, why should not we have seen them? As a matter of fact—I don't speak for Mr. Judge—I did see them, and went up them."

"I, too," said Judge.

"Then we are either all mad together, or something very strange has taken place. Possibly you can tell me where they led to?"

"No; my memory is a blank, till I came down again."

"And you, Mr. Judge?"

"I also remember nothing."

Mrs. Richborough suddenly lost colour, and her breathing grew difficult. She recovered herself by a violent effort.

"You must both have gone up before me, and come down after me. How was that? And how did your ring come to fall down out of the wall? A ring doesn't escape from one's finger of its own accord."

"I cannot answer the conundrum." Isbel's face was like granite.

"If I were an engaged girl, I should not like such a thing to happen to me. Have you *no* idea how it could have happened?"

"No."

"It's very, very strange." Mrs. Richborough essayed a laugh. "If it did not sound absolutely insane, one might almost suppose you had been playing pitch-and-toss with it."

Isbel went white to the lips, but she said nothing.

"You take it very calmly," proceeded the widow. "Let us hope that Mr. Stokes, when he hears. . ."

"Please hold your tongue, Mrs. Richborough! It has nothing whatever to do with you. I've not even told you that it is his ring. You are taking a very great deal for granted."

"You only wore one ring at lunch, my dear, and that was on the third finger of your left hand."

"Very well—then it *is* my engagement ring. What of it? Must I ask your permission before accidentally losing it?"

"I assure you I haven't the slightest wish to interfere in your affairs; still sometimes the advice of an older woman. . ."

"Oh, *advice!* . . . Well, what do you advise?"

"I think it is only good sense to try and find out something more about it. Let us assume that the explanation is *supernatural* . . ."—she looked up with a malicious half-smile—"or can you account for it in someother way?"

"I have already told you that I can't account for it. If you have any useful suggestion to make, please be quick about it."

"I suggest that we all come over here again in the morning and pursue the investigation. I cannot see what else there is to do."

"Why should *you* trouble to come again because I have mysteriously lost and found a ring?"

"Because I wish to," responded Mrs. Richborough, coolly.

"And if I refuse?"

"I shall assume that you consider my society undesirable."

"And. . . ?"

"And act accordingly."

Isbel opened her bag to take out her handkerchief. In doing so, she encountered among its miscellaneous contents a strange envelope. The light in the hall, though fast fading, was still sufficiently strong to read by, and she drew the letter out to see what it was.

It was addressed to Mrs. Richborough.

She turned it about in a puzzled manner. "This appears to be your property. How it comes to be reposing in my bag I have no idea."

The widow took it almost rudely.

"It certainly *is* mine. There's no letter inside—you haven't *that* inside your bag, I suppose?" She searched hurriedly in her own. "It's all right—I have it myself. I'm sorry. But what in the world are you doing with the envelope?"

"There's nothing written on it, by any chance?" suggested Judge thoughtfully.

Mrs. Richborough turned it over to see the back.

"Yes, there is. What led you to inquire?"

"If it's nothing personal, do you mind my looking?"

"I can't make head or tail of it. It's music." She handed it up to Judge, who gazed at it for some moments with a kind of uneasy rumination. Isbel looked over his shoulder.

"I only got that letter by this morning's post, so those notes must have been added since. Who did it?"

Isbel gave an icy smile. "We needn't stare at each other so suspiciously. Its sufficiently obvious what has happened. You wrote it yourself *upstairs,* Mrs. Richborough, and I picked it up and brought it down with me."

"You really think that?"

"I'm convinced of it."

"Then all I can say is we're living in the land of dreams!" . . . Continuing to gaze at the back of the envelope, she started to whistle softly through the roughly-written notes of music. The others listened intently. The tune was unrecognisable, yet there was something strangely perplexing in it. It broke off abruptly in the middle; there was no more written down. They stole questioning glances at each other.

The gloom of the hall deepened. . . Suddenly, the fragment of air which Mrs. Richborough had just whistled was repeated by a distant stringed instrument, which seemed to possess very much the vibrating timbre and deep register of a double bass. It continued to carry the theme to its proper ending. The sound appeared to come from a very long way off, for though quite clear it was extraordinarily faint; it gave them the impression of being high over their heads, but, for all that, seemed to belong to the house. . . it lasted for littler longer than a minute, then everything went back to silence.

Judge stood looking as though he were still unable to grasp what had happened, Isbel's white face bore a peculiar smile, but Mrs. Richborough was obliged to take deep and rapid breaths to prevent herself from swooning again. She sat erect in her chair, holding on to the arms.

"What was that?" demanded Judge at last.

"It reopens everything," replied Isbel.

"What do you mean?"

"It looks as if they do not mean to leave us alone. We are not to be allowed to go back, so we must go on. So be it! I am content."

"I don't understand you."

"I think you do, but it doesn't matter."

"I must ask you to speak more clearly, Miss Loment."

"It is not what I say, or what I do, but what is being decided for us. Mrs. Richborough was quite right—we must come here again tomorrow."

"Please take me outside," murmured the widow weakly. Judge at once moved to her assistance, but the girl stepped in between.

"Wait a minute! . . ." She faced Judge. "Do you think things can stop here? Have you no manhood at all? What do you imagine it all means?"

"I must refuse to take the responsibility of inviting you to this house again, Miss Loment." He attempted to speak with firmness but his voice trembled. "If we go on—as you call it—nothing but unpleasantness awaits us; that is manifest. In the meantime, we ought to hurry home as fast as possible. She is seriously unwell."

Mrs. Richborough really looked ghastly. He hastily produced his flask again, which this time she did not refuse. After swallowing a portion of the contents she felt better.

"I shall be quite well in the morning, Mr. Judge," she managed to say the next minute. "Perhaps there will be no great pleasure in coming here again, but we have all a duty to perform. Miss Loment's whole future happiness may be involved."

He eyed her sternly. "What makes you say that?"

"I am neither more intelligent than you, Mr. Judge, not more enlightened; there is not the slightest necessity for me to explain my words. I insist upon our all coming here tomorrow morning."

"You *insist?*"

"That's what I said. I will not consent to leave things in their present uncertainty. I also am implicated in a certain degree. If you really refuse, I shall have to consider where my further duty lies."

"That is plain enough language, I think, Mr. Judge," said Isbel, dryly. "You had better accept. It is the smaller of two evils."

Judge looked at her, but made no reply. He offered his arm to Mrs. Richborough, and she at last got up from her chair.

They quitted the hall. The two women took their places in the car. After locking the house door, Judge approached Isbel to ascertain her wishes with regard to being set down. At her request he consulted his time-table to discover if there were a convenient train from Shoreham. He found one which would not involve an unreasonable detention at the station, and it was arranged that she should alight there.

He was then about to leave her, to take his own seat, when she pulled quietly at his sleeve.

"What are you feeling?" she asked in a low voice.

"You must know."

"Tell me one thing—you haven't altered towards me?"

"No, I haven't altered."

"You have been so cold. You don't wish to break off our. . . friendship?"

Judge worked his jaw, pouched his mouth, and looked away.

"No, I don't wish it; but perhaps it will be necessary."

"You are made of stone, I think. But I'm coming here tomorrow."

"Very well—if it can be arranged. I strongly doubt whether she will be fit."

"And if she isn't?"

"That is a question which answers itself, Miss Loment."

"I'm coming over to Worthing by the same train, in any case. Expect me. . . You don't altogether *despise* me, do you?"

"*Hush!*" . . . He nodded significantly towards Mrs. Richborough. "How could I?"

"Oh, she doesn't hear. Her eyes are closed. Then you will wait for me tomorrow?"

"Yes."

"With or without her, we must go. . . There's nothing else you wish to say to me now?"

"Nothing."

"You are sure?"

"Quite sure."

Isbel sighed, as she sank back on the cushioned seat. Two minutes later they started down the drive.

XVIII

A CATASTROPHE

After a miserable, feverish night of tossing and turning, Isbel at last fell asleep in the early hours of the morning. She awoke again at eight, and at once got up. She felt dull and stupid, was incapable of quickening her movements, her eyes gave her a sense of being sunk half way in her head. So sluggish was her blood that whatever she chanced to look at seemed to possess the power of detaining her gaze for an indefinite period, though all the time she was not really seeing it. To crown all, she had a gnawing toothache. She was deeply depressed.

She dared not think of Judge, yet all her preparations were made with the single view of journeying to Worthing that morning immediately after breakfast. What was to come of her visit, she did not know. Perhaps nothing at all; perhaps it might be the beginning of a new life.

After dressing, and before going downstairs, she stood awhile at the window. It was a still, grey, dismal morning, which threatened to turn to fog or fine rain. It was neither cold nor warm. She contemplated the engagement ring on her finger, playing with it, as she smiled queerly. It was a pretty toy, and all her friends were very pleased with her for wearing it, but. . . supposing she was not destined to wear it any longer? Who could tell what this day was appointed to bring forth, whether for good or for evil? What a quaint surprise for her little circle if it were to prove that, after all, she had rich, red blood in her veins, and not rose-water!

Oh, she did not know *what* she felt! It could not be *passion.* She was conscious of no thrill, but, on the contrary, was thoroughly cold, dull, and despondent. But neither was she playing a part. Something called to her, and that silent voice was irresistible. It was something in *that house. . .* It was like the call of a *drug;* she was a drug-maniac. . . But why Judge? And why that ring yesterday? *Could* it be passion? . . . A passion which kept flaming up, and slumbering again? . . .

Each following day she found it harder to keep away from him. It was not his person, it was not his intellect, it was not his character; it could not be compatibility. . . Then what was it? What was this subtle attraction which was proving so increasingly overwhelming? Was it that, underneath person, intellect, character, there was something else—something which never came to the surface, but disclosed itself only to the *something else* in her? And was all love of this nature, or was it exceptional, prodigious? . . .

Whom to ask? Who loved nowadays? Betrothals and marriages she saw all around her, but if it wasn't money, it was sexual admiration—she could see nothing else. Might not that secret, incomprehensible impulse which drew her to him be more worthy of the name of *love* than these despicable physical infatuations of worldly men and women? . . .

At ten o'clock she left the hotel, procured a taxi on the front, and within a quarter of an hour was standing inside the booking-hall at Hove Station.

It was not yet half-past eleven as she mounted the steps of the Metropole. She swept through the door, and approached the office window, assuming an air of *hauteur* which was contradicted by the trembling of her hands, as she fumbled in her bag for her card-case. Producing a card, she passed it over the counter to the lady clerk.

"Will you please have that sent up to Mrs. Richborough?"

The clerk looked at the card, and at her. She said nothing, but went to consult with someone else, who was out of sight; Isbel could hear them whispering together. Presently the girl came back, and requested her to accompany her to another room, adjoining the office. Isbel did so. She was begged to sit down, and then left to her own society, the door being closed upon her. It was all very solemn and mysterious.

A minute afterwards a well-dressed man of middle age entered the room. He had a florid German-looking face, and a bald forehead; he was wearing braided trousers, with an irreproachable frock-coat. Isbel took him to be the hotel manage.

"You are Miss Loment, madam?" he asked with suave gravity, gazing at the card in his hand.

She replied in the affirmative.

"You are inquiring for Mrs. Richborough?"

Isbel had risen to her feet.

"Yes; I wish to see her."

"You are a relative, madam?"

"Oh, no. Why?"

"It is my regrettable duty to inform you that Mrs. Richborough was taken suddenly ill in her room last night, and died almost immediately afterwards. A medical man fortunately was in attendance."

"Oh, good heavens! . . ." Isbel grasped the chair-back to steady herself.

"The precise time was 9.15. It was very sudden, and very sad. . . Naturally, we are anxious that this should not be known among the other guests. I feel sure that I can rely upon your discretion, madam."

"Oh, what a tragedy! . . . But surely Mr. Judge know of it?"

"Yes, Mr. Judge does know."

"Could I speak to him a minute, please? Will you send my name up?"

"I regret that it is impossible, madam. Mr. Judge left us this morning."

"*Left* you? . . . Do you mean he has gone away—altogether?"

"Yes, madam; he has returned to London."

"But—has he taken his things with him? Isn't he coming back?"

"No, he is not coming back. . . One moment, madam. . ." He consulted the card in his hand. "I believe he has left a letter for you in charge of the office. If you will pardon me, I will go and inquire."

Isbel could not even find words to thank him. She sat down, feeling as if the roof had fallen upon her. She understood that a catastrophe had happened, but she was unable to realise its final significance.

It was the clerk who brought the letter in, a moment or two later. She handed it to Isbel with a pleasant smile, and instantly retired.

She broke the seal with clumsy haste. The letter ran as follows:

My dear Miss Loment

"I am sorry to inform you that Mrs. Richborough died suddenly last night of heart failure. The doctor who attended her earlier in the evening had ordered her to bed, and she went there, but a little while late, according to her maid's evidence, she insisted upon rising in order to write an urgent letter, which letter she further insisted upon posting in the hotel box with her own hand. The additional strain upon her lowered vitality which this entailed evidently proved too much for her, for half an hour afterwards she was discovered lying in a dying condition in her room. There will of course be an inquest.

"Under the sad circumstances, I feel that any meeting between us would be improper—doubtless you will agree with me. I have accordingly made my arrangements to return at once to town, and by the time you receive this letter—assuming that you have made your promised visit to Worthing—I shall be already on my way back there.

"I think it will be wise if we allow a considerable time to elapse before attempting to see one another again. We have both, I am afraid, acted rather more impulsively than is altogether consistent with worldly prudence, and, to put it at the lowest, an interval for reflection and a cool weighing of the whole situation will certainly not harm either of us. You will understand, of course, that I blame myself far more than you for the unfortunate happenings of the past few days.

"I am leaving my town address with the hotel people should you desire to write me a line in reply. I do not ask it.

"I do not say adieu, for I sincerely hope that at some future time we shall see a great deal of each other.

"Believe me to be, my dear Miss Loment, your earnest friend and well-wisher.

Henry Judge

After flashing through the letter from beginning to end, to extract its message, Isbel allowed it to slip from her hand, while she sat back with close eyes... Then she picked it up again, and twice re-read it, word by word. During the perusal her bosom rose and sank the blood mounting to her face, and once or twice she laughed...

Crushing the sheets into her hand-bag, she closed it with an angry snap.

So *that* was over! . . .

The manager escorted her to the outer door. At the foot of the hotel steps she came to a standstill, not knowing in the least what to do, or where to go. She caught sight of an elegantly dressed lady, in expensive furs, who was in the act of entering a closed car not five yards away from where she was standing. The chauffeur was taking his final instructions, preparatory to assuming his seat. The lady's back was towards her, but somehow her figure struck a familiar chord.

" . . . But first of all, Runhill Court," said the unknown, as she stooped to get in.

Isbel felt bemused. It was not the destination named which dismayed her faculties, and made her feel as though she were in a dream—though this destination was extraordinary enough, in all conscience—but the intonation with which the words were uttered. That sweet, sinking whisper belonged only to one person of her acquaintance, and she could not conceive a second voice like it in the world. It was Mrs. Richborough's. . .

As the car drove off she obtained a single rapid glimpse of the lady's face. Mrs. Richborough was dead, and therefore it could not be she; but, then, it must be her twin sister. The resemblance was absolutely uncanny. . . Well, it was not difficult to understand why a sister should be there at such a distressful time—but what in the world was she doing at Runhill? What possible interest could she have in that house? Evidently some mystery was afoot. . . Could it be that Judge had arranged a meeting with her there in order to talk over the affairs of her late sister? But what affairs could there be to discuss between them? And why select that out-of-the-way spot for the interview? What did it all mean? . . .

She turned to the smart-looking young hotel door-porter, who still stood gazing after the car. "Who *is* that lady?"

"Lady Brooke, miss."

"Is she in anyway related to the late Mrs. Richborough, do you know?"

"I've never seen them together, miss, and I should say it's very unlikely. Lady Brooke is a very exclusive lady."

"She did tell the chauffeur Runhill Court, didn't she?"

"No, miss—Arundel," was the surprised answer.

Isbel was greatly perplexed, but thought it wise to ask no more questions about her. She inquired for, and was directed to the nearest hiring garage in the neighbourhood of the hotel.

It had entered her mind that she, too, must go to Runhill, though what she expected to accomplish by so doing, she had no idea. . . that the door-porter must have received certain instructions—or, perhaps he had mistaken the person she had referred to. She *knew* that it was either Mrs. Richborough or her twin sister. And she *knew* that that woman had said "Runhill Court." It was absolutely necessary and important that she should follow her there, to see what was on foot. . . And, of course, Mr. Judge must be waiting for her there. . . and it was all lies! lies! lies!

She was lucky in getting a landaulette at once. Money was of no account to her, she agreed to the charge demanded without demur, and within five minutes was on her way.

The car was badly sprung, and jolted her abominably; the cushions stank of oil; her tooth started to ache again. Although it was not actually raining, the day was gloomy and forbidding, and everything seemed saturated with damp. Water dripped from the trees. The roads were greasy and they kept skidding. Not a single gleam of light sky promised better things. Isbel squeezed herself in a corner, and closed her eyes.

After passing Steyning, she roused herself. The chauffeur seemed an utter idiot—his work was in this part of the country, and yet he was forever pulling up to ask her for directions. She told him as well as she could. . . Would this terrible journey never come to an end? . . .

At last they reached the lane which ran past the lodge. Here the road forked. One lane went by the lodge; the other, which she did not know, appeared to skirt the western boundary of the estate, going due north somewhere. The chauffeur stopped the car once more at this fork, and Isbel was about to direct him to proceed straight forward when suddenly her eyes rested on a fashionably-dressed woman in furs, who was walking quickly but delicately up the second lane, away from them. She was about twenty yards ahead, and was alone. . . it was *she* . . . So he *had* lied, that porter! . . . But, oh heavens! what an appalling resemblance to Mrs. Richborough. She could pick up that step out of a thousand others. . . Then she *wasn't* dead. The whole thing was a conspiracy, directed against her, Isbel. Judge had fallen a victim to that woman at last, and they were quietly putting her out of the way, as an inconvenient person. The hotel manager had been bribed. There was really nothing left to explain. . .

"You needn't come any further. I'm getting out." Isbel suited the action to the word.

The man looked dissatisfied. "Am I to wait?"

"No, you can go home. Do I pay you, or the garage?"

Being a casual hirer, she had to pay him. She hurriedly gave him notes to cover the charge, and, without waiting for the change, or interesting herself in his further movements, at once turned her back on him and started quickly up the lane, round the bend of which the unknown woman had by this time vanished.

She reached the bend herself. The disagreeable noise of the departing car grew fainter and fainter as the distance increased between them, until finally she heard no sounds but those of nature. Everything around her was moist, dripping, and sullen. . . Mrs. Richborough—for she had now no doubt that it was she—was still a considerable distance in front. They were both walking swiftly, so there was no question of catching her up. Isbel did not quite understand where she was going to, but probably there was another way into the grounds from this side, which would obviate the necessity of passing through the lodge-gate. . . But, if so, how had that woman come to know of it? And, by the way, where had *her* car disappeared to? . . . Isbel asked herself many questions during that period, but she was unable to answer anyone of them.

The whole right-hand side of the lane was bordered by an ancient, red brick wall which bounded the estate. Beyond it was a park, looking grey and disconsolate enough on such a day as this; the wet grass was knee-high, and every faintest breath of wind brought water off the brown-leaved trees. The park sloped downhill from the lane at first, but presently it became level. A dark grey shadowy mass on the forward right was probably the house itself; very likely it was not so far away as it looked, but the light was so bad. . . Suddenly half way along a straight stretch of lane, her quarry vanished. . .

Isbel was careful to keep her eye on the spot where she had last observed her. No doubt there would be an entrance there into the grounds.

Upon coming up to it she found her anticipation was realised. A small iron wicket-gate opened into the park. It had been swung to, but was unlatched. A gravel walk, barely wide enough for two people side by side, led through the grass and under trees towards what could now distinctly be seen to be the house. It was slightly uphill. Isbel passed in without hesitation.

After walking quickly for about five minutes, she again saw the woman. She was as far ahead as ever. She had reached the foot of the steep sloping lawn under the house, and now turned sharply to the left, which would evidently bring her to the north-east side of the building— though how she could be so certain of her direction on this, her first visit to the grounds, was more than Isbel could say. The house itself was by this time quite close. Standing high above her, in the grey mist, it looked a huge, weird erection, the more especially as it was a mere silhouette. The part which faced her must be the back—the French windows of the dining-room, the bedrooms of the top storey, etc. . . But by the time that Isbel had gained the same spot, beneath the lawn, the woman had again disappeared. She also turned to the left.

The path curved, and in another minute or two she was in full view of the north-east front. The lawn, which was still steeper on this side, towered above her in that dim visibility like a veritable mountain slope, and crowning it was the great house, vast, shadowy, and grim. She could just make out the gable underneath which was the window of the East Room.

While she paused to gaze up, she became aware that the woman was standing close beside her. Then her doubts were remove. It *was* Mrs. Richborough! . . . there was something disquieting and peculiar in her appearance, however. . . Perhaps it was the way she was standing. Her hands were free, and they crossed, not over her breast but over the lower part of her body, with straightened elbows. She was also very erect and still. Her face appeared white and smiling, under the decorative veil she wore—but perhaps it was illusion, the light was so poor. Isbel felt a strange uneasiness.

"They told me at the hotel that—something happened to you."

"Oh, yes—I *am dead,*" came the whispering voice. "I died last night."

And then Isbel realised that her eyes were closed, that this being standing opposite to her, with the dress and bearing of a fashionable woman, did not see the world as other people! . . .

Her tongue was paralysed, and she shook from head to foot.

The apparition vanished.

XIX

The Flash of Day

The mist came on thicker. It was so wetting that her clothes and face streamed with moisture, though she was too distressed to think of seeking shelter. The upper lawn appeared as a dark shadow against the paler grey of the sky, while the house itself was out of sight.

As she stood trying to overcome her agitation, something began to affect her ears. It was not exactly a sound, but was more like a heavy pulsing. Her head throbbed with it, till she thought she should go mad. Then it ceased abruptly.

Five minutes later, the figure of a man loomed up out of the mist and approached her. It was Judge. Isbel pressed her fur tightly to her throat and turned away.

"So it is you!"

When he replied, there was a suppressed exuberance in his voice which immediately arrested her attention by its unusualness.

"Yes, it is I."

"Then you told me an untruth? You have not gone to London?"

"I called here on my way back."

"Well, I got your letter. Perhaps you are wondering why I have followed you here, after having received my dismissal. I don't want anything from you, and I don't know myself why I came. Mrs. Richborough led me here. I know now that she's dead, but I have seen her and spoken to her, for all that."

Judge seemed not to remark her statement, for he asked another question:

"Did you hear my playing?"

"Your playing?"

"Yes." . . . He eyed her curiously. "Your manner is very extraordinary. Surely you recognise where you are? Are you awake or asleep?"

"I'm quite awake and I fully realise where I am, Mr. Judge. I'm trespassing in your grounds—but it won't be for long. I'm going home now."

"Haven't you been to the house?"

"Your house? Hardly, I think."

He drew a step closer, and for the first time she observed that he was not wearing a hat.

"Tell me where you think you are?"

"I have already told you. It is *your* manner which is very singular, Mr. Judge. Are you quite well?"

"Listen! I am talking with you here, and I am where we wished to be yesterday. Does it not seem so to you, too?"

"I don't understand you. Where did we wish to be yesterday?"

He gave her another searching look. "So you really are seeing differently. And you have not been up that staircase today?"

"I haven't set foot inside your house, I tell you. Have you lost your senses?"

"No; but I *have* been up that staircase today, and I have not yet come down again."

"Oh, my God!" said Isbel quietly.

"I was wretched, and could not keep away from the house. It contained all my memories. The stairs were there; I climbed them. Passing straight into that other room, I got through the window, and succeeded in reaching the ground without accident, though it was not easy. . ."

She stared at him with frightened eyes. "And where are you now?"

"I am standing beside you in the open country, in full sunshine—and it is spring, not autumn."

"You cannot believe it. You must see for yourself that it isn't so. Feel me—I'm wet with the fine rain."

But he came no nearer.

"The man is asleep, and the sight of his instrument put an idea into my head. I could not see you, but I felt you were somewhere in the neighbourhood—so I played to you. . ."

"What man?"

"The man we saw from the window yesterday."

There was an embarrassed silence.

"But this is awful!" said Isbel. . . "You must be attempting to mystify me, Mr. Judge. If not. . ."

"No, I am speaking the truth, Isbel; and I am quite rational."

The blood came to her face. "You have not yet acquired the right to call me by that name, Mr. Judge."

"You don't understand—but matters can be set right."

"Where are you now going?"

He had started to move off, but stopped at her question.

"I shall play again."

"But this is sheer insanity."

"You did not think so last evening, when we heard that music in the hall."

She said nothing.

"Let me go," proceeded Judge quietly. "I ask you only to reserve your judgement for five minutes, and in the meantime to wait here. Should I fail to open your eyes by then, I give you full permission to think of me what you will. Please wait."

Isbel stared after him with a puzzled frown, as he made his way up and across the long, wet grass. He had hardly taken ten steps before his form merged into the grey of the mist and was swallowed up. She heard nothing but the dripping of the sodden trees.

While waiting, with a fast-beating heart, for the outcome of this strange business, she experienced the same sensations in her ears as before. It was an inaudible throbbing, too marked to be disregarded, but so unassociated that she was unable even to decide if its cause were internal or external. After continuing for a minute or two, it left off as suddenly as it had started. Nearly at the same time she was surprised to see the day rapidly brightening. The sky grew lighter, and the mists thinner; she could look further away each moment. In less than five minutes after Judge's departure the sun itself had come through. The blue sky appeared, the ground vapours dispersed, and the whole country became visible. The transition was so abrupt that she scarcely knew how to take it; almost in a flash, to the radiance and heat of an early summer day. A wind sprang up, and long before she had accommodated herself to the change there was not a wisp of cloud in the sky. She loosened her fur wrap.

She was standing in the same attitude—looking up towards the house. Suddenly a shock passed through her system. She had just realised the house was *gone*. It had vanished, absolutely and entirely. And not only the house, but its grounds as well, including the very lawn on which her foot had been resting. . . She discovered herself to be on the side of a steep, grassy hill, through the turf of which the naked chalk showed. She was some way down from the top, but there was not the least room for doubt that there was no building there; its bare ridge joined the sky from end to end. . . Here was a miracle indeed! . . .

Upon turning swiftly to see what was behind her, she was bewildered to meet the identical panorama which she and Judge had viewed yesterday from that window. The hillside she stood on was where the strangely-dressed man had been; she recognised at once by its general configuration and relation to the landscape. The sharp, smooth slope descended to the same little valley, along which flowed the same little brook; beyond it was that other hill, with the unbroken forest stretching to the horizon. . . after staring for a few moments, she clapped her hand to her eyes, and cried out. She could not understand it, and she feared she was on the point of losing her reason. But when she looked again she saw the same things, down to the smallest detail, and all was so brightly-coloured, so solid, so *real* in appearance, that she could not hesitate any longer to accept the scene as being actually existent. . . And it was so beautiful! The forest trees were clothed in fresh green leaves, the smaller trees in the valley underneath were smothered with white blossom, song-birds trilled and twittered, a wood pigeon was cooing softly, two distant cuckoos seemed to be answering each other, high overhead a lark fluttered and sang. The caressing wind brought to her the rich, moist fragrance of the whole countryside. . . Yes, yes—it was spring! . . .

She remembered everything. Every particular of her three visits to those other rooms at Runhill returned to her with startling distinctness, so that she was amazed how she could ever have forgotten. Moreover, her whole relation to Henry, both in private and in public, was suddenly made clear. She saw how worldly prudence on his side, angry pride on hers, had nearly succeeded in wrecking their happiness, and how this state of affairs had arisen, not from any fault of character on either part, not from any insufficiency of love, but from pure ignorance of the fact. They had not known that they *belonged* to each other. . .

Her heart sang as she saw him approaching her from higher up. He was only a short distance away. Still further back, behind him, she caught a glimpse of the gaily-dressed musician. He was lying on his side, head uphill, back towards her, apparently asleep; his fiddle-shaped instrument was beside him. Isbel gave him a silent welcome, but at that moment Henry was the more wonderful vision of the two. She had no real eyes for anything but him.

They hastened to each other with outstretched hands.

"You heard me this time?" laughed Henry, enfolding her and looking down into her eyes.

"My ears throbbed—was that really you? . . . Oh, Henry, what a terribly narrow escape we've had! How could we have been so absolutely insane? Surely we must have know that that ring was not thrown away for nothing? . . ."

"Some kind fate is watching over us, evidently. Whether we deserve it by our stupidity is quite another matter. . . However, you see now I'm not so mad as you thought I was?"

"It's heaven, I think. But is it true? . . . Where has the house gone to?"

"We're in the house."

Even while they were speaking, the brightness of the day began perceptibly to fade, almost as though a solar eclipse were creeping on. The sun became obscured by haze, the blue of the sky grew paler and paler, thin mists commenced again to crawl about the lower regions. The wind dropped, and a sort of hush came over the scene. The birds sang more fitfully.

"It's getting darker," whispered Isbel, with a slight shiver, uneasily drawing her fur closer to her.

"No, no. Dismiss the possibility. It can't change now." His strong-featured face smiled down at her protectingly.

"Let's hope not. . . How do you mean—'we're in the house'?"

"I entered it from the grounds, and I haven't passed out again into the grounds, therefore I'm still in it—and you're with me. I don't profess to understand, but it is so, and it can't be otherwise."

The mist sensibly thickened. Isbel could scarcely distinguish the trees on the opposite side of the valley. The sun disappeared, the sky was a whitish grey, while the air felt cold and damp.

"Henry, I'm going!" she said, quietly detaching herself from his embrace. . . "Everything's falling back. . ."

His face fell in alarm. "What's the matter? What's happening to you? . . ."

"We're returning to the old state. The sun's gone in, and it's growing misty and cold. . . Oh, can't you see it?"

"No, I can't. There's no difference at all—the day is as glorious as ever it was. . . Exert your will! . . ."

"My mind is getting all mixed up, too. I seem to be losing my grip of things. . . Do you know, I can hardly remember yesterday?"

"My poor, poor girl! Make an effort. Force yourself to see that it isn't so."

"Unfortunately, one cannot conquer facts. Oh, I'm going back right enough. It's been a short-lived dream this time—but it doesn't signify."

Judge bit his nails in agitation. "What's to be done? Something must be done. I must think of something. . ."

"I verily believe you are more concerned than I," she replied smiling. "You had better wake that man. Is he still lying there? I can no longer see."

"Wake him?"

"Is he too terrible to be waked?"

"His face is buried in his arm."

"Perhaps he will help us. He has done so before. But be quick! It will soon be too late."

"I'll go at once. May it turn out well! There's something very unusual in his appearance."

By that time both the crest of the hill and the valley beneath were blotted out. She was unable to see for more than a few feet around her, while the mist resembled a fine, driving rain, which did its work none the less effectually because it was impalpable.

She signed to Judge to stop, and, after staring at him for a few moments, with knitted brows, said:

"I'm afraid I've lost the thread of my ideas. Of whom are we speaking?"

"Of that man. The musician."

"What man? What musician?"

"Isbel! . . ."

"Mr. Judge," she said quietly, "my head is very confused, and I have to plead guilty to not remembering what or whom we were talking about; but one thing I do recollect. I requested you a short time ago to address me with the same courtesy which you would use towards any other lady of your acquaintance."

Judge turned pale, and bowed.

"You left me a few minutes ago," she went on, "and it seems you've come back. Is there any advantage to be gained by our pursuing this conversation?"

"I have no explanation to offer which you would at present be able to understand. I will absent myself once more. Please be good enough to wait here a few moments longer. I have complete confidence that everything will be made clear to you."

His features bore an expression of earnestness and humility which succeeded only in still further irritating her.

"No, I'm going home. Your conduct ever since yesterday, Mr. Judge, is entirely beyond my comprehension, but I will put the most charitable construction upon it that I can, and give you a word of advice. Continue your journey to London with as little delay as possible, and lose no time in seeking your medical adviser."

Judge bowed again.

"I think we shall not see one another again," proceeded Isbel. "I will take this opportunity of saying goodbye. It has been a very. . . *broken* friendship."

Without waiting for any further speech from him, she started slowly to mount the lawn, having no definite plans for getting back to Brighton, but feeling that she would gain her bearings better from the house in the first place. She did not trust herself to retrace the route by which she had come. The thick, white, rolling vapours shut her in, as in a prison. . . Judge, standing there in brilliant sunshine and an atmosphere which showed everything as clear-cut and painted, saw her one moment, and failed to see her the next. She had disappeared before his eyes. He made a gesture of dismay, and began in hot haste to scramble up the hillside obliquely, in the direction of the sleeping musician.

Isbel heard a long, low, scraping sound, like the slow drawing of a bow across the low string of a deep-toned viol. It was succeeded by silence.

She was by this time close up to the house, and she looked towards it, but was unable to understand where she had come to. It was a different building. As well as could be distinguished through the mist, it was constructed entirely of unpainted timber, from top to bottom; the roof was flat, without gables, and there appeared to be four storeys. Then the fog shut out the vision again.

A strange warmth was running through her body. All her other sensations seemed to be merged in the recollection that she was a *woman* . . . Fever was abroad in the air, and her blood grew hotter and hotter. . .

That musical noise returned, but now the note was low, fierce, passionate, exactly resembling a deep, forced human cry of love-pain. . .

Everything happened in a single second. Between twin periods of fog and gloom, came one flash of summer sunlight. It entered upon her with the abrupt unexpectedness of a stroke, and before she realised where she was, or what had happened to her, it had departed again leaving her stunned and terrified. Meanwhile, this is what she seemed to see. She was standing in sunshine again, on that bare hill, gazing at the distant forest, across the valley. The sky was cloudless. She was nearly at the top of the hill, and the house had vanished. . . She recollected everything, but could settle to nothing. Her mood was one of unutterable excitement and reckless audacity; she appeared to herself to be laughing and sobbing under her breath. . .

Henry and that other man were facing each other on the hillside, a little way below her. The man was tall and stout, and, in his bright-coloured, archaic garments, cut an extraordinary figure. He held his instrument against his chest, and was in the act of drawing his bow across it—the note she had heard had not yet come to an end. His back was turned towards her, so that she could not see his face, but Henry, who was standing erect and motionless beyond, was looking right into it, and, from his expression, it was as though he were beholding some appalling vision! . . . She screamed and ran towards him, calling him by name. Before she had taken three steps, however, the musician jerked his whole force savagely into his bow-arm, and she was brought up with a violent shock. Such sharp brutality of passion she had never heard expressed by any sound. . . The sunlight grew suddenly hotter and darker, the landscape appeared to close rapidly in upon her, some catastrophe was impending; her blood was boiling and freezing. . .

At that moment it seemed to her that yonder strange man was the centre around which everything in the landscape was moving, and that she herself was no more than *his* dream! . . .

And then Henry's face was crossed by an expression of sickness; he changed colour; she caught a faint groan, and directly afterwards he sank helplessly to the ground, where he continued lying quite still. . . she stood paralysed, staring in horror. . .

The sunlight vanished instantaneously. Everything was grey and cold again, the sky was leaden; she saw nothing but driving rain-mists. . . She rubbed her eyes with her knuckles, wondering what had occurred, how she came to be standing there, as in a dream, why she felt so sick and troubled? . . .

Then she quietly fainted where she stood.

XX

Marshall's Journey

On arriving at Lloyd's at ten o'clock on the same morning, Marshall found among his letters a typewritten envelope of uncommercial size and shape. Out of curiosity, he opened it the first. The communication enclosed was typed on small, feminine notepaper, and was neither addressed nor signed. It was, in fact, anonymous. Before reading it, he turned again to the envelope, to inspect the postmark. It was stamped Worthing. The only person he could think of as staying at Worthing was Judge.

He read the following words:

"If Mr. Stokes is interested to know how Miss L—spends her time during his temporary absences, it might be as well for him to inquire at Runhill Court. There is every reason to believe that she will be there tomorrow (Friday) morning before lunch, for the *third time this week*, and he may consider the matter of sufficient importance to justify his presence there on the same occasion. Should it not be *before* lunch, it may be *after*. It is believed that there are rooms in the house which are not easy to discover."

Marshall carefully folded the letter, and deposited it in his pocket-case. Then he sat back, and began to slowly pass his hand over his eyes and forehead.

His first impulse was to ignore the whole business, destroy the note, and say nothing about it to Isbel or anyone else. To start testing the accuracy of a charge, of which, naturally, he did not believe a single word, would be equivalent to admitting that there might be a possibility of truth in it, and that would be a ghastly insult to Isbel. . .

But then there was the question of libel. Some ill-disposed person—probably a woman—was evidently bent on mischief, and it was doubtful how far she would go if no counter-action was taken. The thing obviously was to find out, in the first place, who wrote the letter. The police were out of the question, and private inquiry agents were not much better; he did not intend to have her name bandied about by these professional gentlemen. She herself was the only one who might be able to throw light on the business. He would show her the letter that same evening when he went down to Brighton, and they would talk it over together. A person who was prepared to go to that criminal length did not spring out of empty space—Isbel would have a tolerable idea who it was, and why she, or he, had done it. . .

Of course, spite was at the bottom of it. But what he could not quite see through was the explicit character of the charge. Where was the sense of quoting time and place, when the writer must be aware that any action taken on the statement would expose the whole damned lie? Probably it was a bit of low cunning. It was thought that he would *not* take action, and that the poison would continue to rankle in his mind. . . That seemed all right as far as he could see. And in that case he was not at all sure that it might not be good policy to make the move he was not expected to make. Of course, before going to Runhill, to see what game was on foot, he would look Isbel up at Brighton, and very likely take her with him.

He made hurried arrangements with his deputy to carry on during his absence, and immediately afterwards left for Victoria.

It was not long after noon when he arrived at the Gondy Hotel. Mrs. Moor gave an exclamation of surprise when she saw him.

"Good gracious, Marshall!—what can this mean?"

He told a story of having met a man. . . "Where's Isbel?" he added quickly.

Isbel, it seemed, had been out for two hours, and Mrs. Moor had no idea *where* she was.

In a very decomposed manner, Marshall muttered something about returning later in the day. He took his departure abruptly—almost rudely. She could not think what had come over him. Probably it was some business worry.

Meanwhile Marshall, with a face which grew sterner each minute, sought his car in the hotel garage. While it was being got out, he produced and lit a cigar. He wished to assure himself that his feelings were tranquil, and that the visit to Runhill he was about to make was a quite ordinary, matter-of-fact transaction, of no special consequence, and undertaken merely as a piece of necessary routine work. . . Perhaps he really did not see, perhaps he did not wish to see, that it can never be an ordinary transaction to test a woman's honour. . .

He got in, turned up the collar of his rainproof coat, pulled down his crushed-in hat, and started off. It was a quarter to one. He pushed the car along fast to Shoreham, but, once past the houses, he let her go altogether. . . In just over the half hour he reached Runhill Lodge.

Priday appeared.

Marshall got down. . . "Good afternoon! Is there anyone up at the house?" He had returned the cigar-stump to his mouth when he had spoken.

"The boss is there, sir."

"Mr. Judge?"

"Ah."

"Anyone with him?" The keen glint of his eye, as he threw a side-glance, belied his indifferent tone.

"No, sir, he's by himself. He ain't been there much above half an hour."

Marshall remained silent for a minute.

"I'll walk up to him, I think."

"Shall I open the gate?"

"No, I said I'd *walk* up. The car's quite all right where it is. Thank you, Priday."

He threw away his stump, passed through the side gate, and started slowly up the drive, with bent head. Priday, after gazing after him for a short time, disappeared again inside the lodge. The dismal, wetting mist made it no sort of day to be out in.

As he approached the house, Marshall saw a small car standing outside the main entrance. It was evidently Judge's. When he came up to it, he leant over the side, to make a somewhat ashamed, but none the less careful scrutiny of the seats and floor. He hardly dared to confess himself what he feared to see there. It was with heartfelt relief that he failed to detect anything of a compromising character. He crossed to the house. The hall door was unlocked; he opened it, and went straight in.

The hall was grey, sombre, and silent. He wondered which would be the likeliest part of the house to start looking for Judge. . . Nine chances out of ten, he would be upstairs in his favourite lurking-spot— the East Room. It might be good sense to go there first. . . What did that damned correspondence mean by there being rooms hard to find? . . . Oh, hell! Isbel *couldn't* be there. Priday said no one was there except Judge. . . why the devil was he wasting precious time mooning in the hall, when he ought by now to be up at the top of the house? . . .

He made for the main staircase and raced up, three steps at a time. Without pausing on the landing, he immediately attacked the upper flight, and in less than a minute was groping his way through the black darkness of the upstairs corridor.

He saw at once that the door of the East Room was standing open. Upon getting closer he saw something else. A man was lying, huddled and motionless, on the floor, near one of the walls. It required no flash of inspiration to guess that it was Judge—but what had happened to him? Was he asleep, fainting, or drunk? . . . He leapt over to him, and pulled his face round. . . then let go again in horror. The man was dead! . . .

There was no doubt of the fact, and there was little doubt of the cause of death. The discoloured face told its own story—apoplexy! . . . To make quite sure, he tested the heart. After crouching for at least five minutes, with his hand on Judge's naked chest, he saw that it was hopeless to go on—there was not the faintest whisper of a heartbeat.

He did whatever he thought was immediately necessary, then walked away and downstairs, to fetch assistance.

The unexpected tragedy had put his own affair entirely out of his head. He had forgotten Isbel's connection with the house, and, for the moment, almost her very existence. He was too preoccupied with his immediate plans for action to see anything around him; otherwise, upon reaching the head of the main staircase, he would have at once perceived, straight ahead of him, Isbel herself, sitting in a chair near the other end of the hall. As it was, it was not until he was close upon her that he jumped back with a start. . . Her face was white, her eyes were closed, her clothing appeared to be wet and stained with mud, while her whole attitude was one of lassitude and exhaustion.

"Isbel! What does this mean? . . ." He came on again until he nearly stood over her. She opened her eyes slowly and looked up with weary indifference, manifesting no surprise at his presence, nor, indeed, any emotion whatever.

"How did you get here?" was all she asked.

"Never mind me. How did you come to be in this house?"

"I fainted outside, and came in to sit down, before going home."

"Outside? But what were you doing outside? What are you doing in this part of the world at all?"

It was several seconds before she answered.

"Don't be hard on me, Marshall, I can't explain now. . . I have a confession to make—but not now."

He whipped the anonymous letter out of his pocket-case, and handed it to her. "Will you read that?"

She did so, while he watched her closely; his heart sank, as he saw that she showed neither astonishment nor indignation. She read it through twice, quite apathetically, and then passed it back without a word.

"Well? . . ." demanded Marshall.

"I know who wrote that. Is that what you want?"

"Never mind who wrote it. Is it *true?*"

"Perhaps it isn't true; but it was written in good faith. I meant to come here this morning with Mr. Judge, but he disappointed me."

"I see. . . May I ask why. . . ?"—but he was unable to finish.

"Why, I wished to be here with him? . . ." She smiled bitterly. "Please don't press me to give explanation which you won't receive."

There was dead silence.

"Then you haven't seen him today?" asked Marshall.

"I can't say—I don't know. I don't know whom I've seen, and whom I haven't seen. I have fainted. I don't know anything."

"So perhaps you don't know where he is at this moment?"

"That I'll swear to, Marshall. I've only just this minute entered the house for the first time."

"Then I'll tell you. He's upstairs in the East Room" . . . He looked at her, to see if she were as ignorant of the tragedy as her words and manner professed, but she did not even appear interested.

"*Dead,*" he added, suddenly and brutally.

Isbel half-rose from her seat, and turned such a greenish colour that he thought she was about to swoon again, but he did not go to her assistance. She recovered herself by an effort.

"Have you killed him?" she demanded quietly.

"I have not. I don't believe in private assassinations. He has had some sort of fit—and now I'm off to tell Priday and fetch a doctor. . . We had better resume this very interesting conversation later. And if I may venture to offer a suggestion—there will probably be an inquest, and, if you have no special desire to appear among the witnesses, it would be as well for you to lose no time in getting clear of the premises. Does anyone know you're here, barring Judge himself?"

"No."

"Then how did you get in?"

"By another gate."

"Well, take my advice, and go out the same way. Can you find your way on to the main Steyning road?"

"I expect so."

"Then walk on, and I'll pick you up in the car further on. I've got to fetch a doctor, so you'll be there as soon as I shall. . . Go now—don't waste time."

Isbel remained sitting.

"Marshall! . . ."

"What is it?"

"How long has he been dead?"

"Priday says he's only been in the house half an hour. That was fifteen minutes ago, perhaps. He can't have been dead long. Why?"

"Because I feel as if something has snapped inside me since I fell down in that faint. It must have been at the same time. . . Do you think it strange that I don't express a wish to go up and see him?"

"I'm exceedingly sorry, Isbel, but I can't enter into your wishes or feelings. Of course, there's not the slightest need for you to go up, and I strongly advise you not to. . ."

She directed a pitiful smile towards him. "I know there's no going back to the old state. Please don't imagine that I even wish to. I merely want to tell you that perhaps my feelings towards him were not altogether what you think they were. I. . ."

"But you came here to meet him?"

Isbel dived into her hand-bag impulsively. "Marshall, you've shown me a letter; now I'll show you one. . . Read that."

He took it rather unwillingly, and skimmed it through.

"Who is this Mrs. Richborough he speaks about?"

"The person who wrote to you."

"It seems a fatal business all round. And is this letter of Judge's a blind, or did it really extend no further?"

"I wish you to believe that Mr. Judge was a man of honour. . . That's all. Now I'll go. . . I won't insult you by expressing my sorrow for the position I've put you in. . . You have always been good to me, and I'm afraid I've repaid you in the meanest possible way. . . Goodbye, for the time being!"

She got up, and started to stumble towards the door.

"Do you feel yourself able to walk as far as I proposed?" Marshall asked in a singular tone.

She stopped to look back over her shoulder. "It seems to me that I have no alternative."

"That's quite true. I can't come with you, for I have this awful business to attend to. How long will it take you to get clear of the grounds by the way you're going?"

"I don't know—ten minutes. . ."

"I'll sit here for ten minutes by my watch, and then make my way to the lodge. Walk on towards Steyning, and, if I haven't picked you up by the time you have reached there, wait for me at the station. Is that clear?"

"Yes, Marshall."

"Incidentally, how did you get here?"

"By hired car form Worthing, but I dismissed the driver short of the house."

"All right, then—you'd better clear off."

He sat down in the chair which she had vacated, and pulled out his watch. Isbel hesitated a moment, as if she wished to say something more, then a flash of anger at her own weakness seemed to come across her, for she suddenly straightened herself, and walked directly to the door.

Ten minutes later Marshall rose, left the house, and started down the drive towards the lodge.

It was nearing four o'clock when he and Isbel returned to the Gondy together. Isbel went straight to her room. Marshall sought Mrs. Moor, and, without beating around the bush, informed her that the engagement was broken off, by mutual agreement. He referred her to Isbel for all explanations. She was greatly upset, but had too much good sense to attempt to combat his decision there and then, without learning more about the affair. She wished him godspeed, and begged him, with tears in her eyes, at least to leave the road open for future negotiations. However, he declined to make any kind of promise, or to discuss things with her at all. . . He spent the night at the hotel, but dined out, and retired to his room early. On the following morning he packed his belongings, settled his bill, and started back to town in the car, without having attempted previously to see Mrs. Moor for the purpose of saying farewell.

The inquest was held on Tuesday. Marshall was called upon to give evidence as to the finding of the body, but everything was purely formal. The medical witness certified that death was due to cerebral hemorrhage, and the jury returned their verdict accordingly. Isbel did not attend.

The two ladies returned to Kensington, as arranged, in the middle of the week. Isbel refused to discuss matters with her aunt, or to see any of her friends. Blanche behaved with great tact; she neither wrote to her, nor called, but she was continually sending flowers and kind messages by way of Mrs. Moor, and Isbel was not ungrateful. . . a few weeks afterwards, aunt and niece went to the Riviera.

BLANCHE THOUGHT THE OCCASION PROPITIOUS to resume a correspondence with her friend, and Isbel acquiesced, though without any particular pleasure. The first letters were very correct, but, as time passed, Marshall's name began to appear on Blanche's side with greater frequency. In the beginning Isbel thought that it was an unintentional blundering against good taste. It was not long before she realised that the thin end of the wedge had become too securely hammered in to be easily dislodged. She passed over the allusions in silence.

Then the time came for them to return home. It was March. " . . . I want to know how we're to stand, Billy," she wrote her friend. "We see a good deal of Marshall in these days. If you happen to run up against him in my house, may I take it that you will behave towards him with common politeness? . . ."

Isbel wrote back: " . . . If Marshall is able to endure my society, I shall certainly be able to endure his. . ."

On the evening of the same day that Blanche received this letter, she showed these lines to Marshall himself. He coloured violently.

"Well—how am I to answer?" she demanded.

"Tell her I'm not quite a savage."

"Is that all?"

"Don't you think we'd better take one step at a time?" asked Marshall.

Blanche smiled, and suddenly grasped his wrist.

THE END

A Note About the Author

David Lindsay (1876–1945) was a British science fiction novelist. Born in London to a Scottish Calvinist family, he excelled as a student at Colfe's School in Lewisham before embarking on a career in insurance. At 40 years of age, he joined the Grenadier Guards to fight in the First World War, eventually rising to the rank of Corporal. After the war, he moved to Cornwall with his wife Jacqueline to pursue life as a professional writer. *A Voyage to Arcturus* (1920), although a commercial flop, would go on to earn praise from both C. S. Lewis and J. R. R. Tolkien. His next novel, *The Haunted Woman* (1922), sold poorly as well, encouraging Lindsay to give up his dream of commercial success in order to produce the stories he wanted to write. Despite this, his ambition flagged by the mid-1930s, no doubt due in part to his strained relationship with Jacqueline and the financial difficulties of managing their boarding house in Brighton. During the Second World War, a German bomb caused considerable damage to their home, the resulting shock from which led to a decline in the author's physical and mental health. Months before the end of the war, he died from an infection that spread from a severe tooth abscess. In the decades since, scholars and writers alike have praised *A Voyage to Arcturus* as one of the twentieth century's finest works of science fiction and fantasy. English novelist and philosopher Colin Wilson dubbed it the "greatest novel of the twentieth century," while film director Clive Barker has called it "an extraordinary work."

A Note from the Publisher

Spanning many genres, from non-fiction essays to literature classics to children's books and lyric poetry, Mint Edition books showcase the master works of our time in a modern new package. The text is freshly typeset, is clean and easy to read, and features a new note about the author in each volume. Many books also include exclusive new introductory material. Every book boasts a striking new cover, which makes it as appropriate for collecting as it is for gift giving. Mint Edition books are only printed when a reader orders them, so natural resources are not wasted. We're proud that our books are never manufactured in excess and exist only in the exact quantity they need to be read and enjoyed.

bookfinity™

Discover more of your favorite classics with Bookfinity™.

- Track your reading with custom book lists.
- Get great book recommendations for your personalized Reader Type.
- Add reviews for your favorite books.
- AND MUCH MORE!

Visit **bookfinity.com** and take the fun Reader Type quiz to get started.

Enjoy our classic and modern companion pairings!

Printed in the USA
CPSIA information can be obtained
at www.ICGtesting.com
JSHW082340140824
68134JS00020B/1790

9 781513 299853